Merlot Murder

A Meadowood Mystery

Nancy M. Wade

Published in the United States

GARNAN Enterprises, LLC of Ohio.

Copyright 2025 by Nancy M. Wade

All Rights Reserved.

ISBN: E979-89919301-23

ISBN: 979-89919301-30

Edited by: Anna Aysen

❀ Created with Vellum

A Meadowood Mystery

Merlot
Murder

CRIME SCENE DO NOT CROSS

Nancy M. Wade

Contents

Chapter One

Vacation Plans

Vacation!

Even the word brought a smile to my face.

I can't believe we're actually going on a real vacation ... the first time in years. Of course, to be fair, it wasn't always possible to plan a formal trip when the boys were babies and with Doug's career being in probationary stages, plus heaven knows how we would have afforded it financially, anyway. But now ... all the fates have smiled on us as we planned at long last a real vacation trip, even if it's only Lake Erie. I couldn't contain my excitement.

"Sugar, you haven't stopped grinning since you opened that door this morning," drawled Anna Thompson, my partner at the A&M Tea Shop. "Are you gonna tell me what's going on or do I have to drag it out of you?"

"Jeez Louise—Anna, wait until I tell you my news! Doug's parents have offered us their condo at Put-in-Bay for a week's vacation stay. We haven't traveled anywhere in ages; this will be so much fun. Harold and Maude bought a condo on South Bass Island as an investment several years ago and they rent it out during the summer months. I couldn't believe my ears when Maude phoned and told Doug we could use it next week. The timing is perfect, albeit last minute. The boys start back to school in three weeks so getting away now is ideal. I don't think the island will be that crowded in late-August," I explained as I worked.

I moved about the Victorian tea shop, collecting dirty cups and saucers, then draped fresh linens onto small bistro tabletops. Lingering aromas of Earl Grey tea and warm spices filled the air. The atmosphere of our shop was quaint and feminine, with its graceful chintz upholstery and curtains. Anna's decorative floral grapevine wreaths adorning the walls added an extra touch. Display cases filled with knit tea cozies, delicate demitasse teacups, and a collection of sugar bowls and creamers tweaked our customer's interest and boosted our sales.

We served a variety of flavorful teas using delicate porcelain tea sets and miniature tea pots. The local bakery across the street, Martha's Delites, was owned by a dear friend. Martha Parker provided delicious scones for our customers' delight. We supplemented our sweet offerings with muffins and cookies that Anna and I baked in the shop's kitchen. The addition of petite tea sandwiches completed our daily menu. For over a year or so, we had devoted all our energy to growing and marketing our enterprise, and now the quaint tea shop was a popular tourist attraction in Meadowood.

We'd had another busy day at the tea shop. Now, with the closed sign in place, Anna and I went about our chores of straightening up, washing dishes, and preparing the next day's menu and food preparation. We worked so well together; our routine had become a well-choreographed ballet.

"Sounds wonderful. Wish Chuck and I could get away; we both need the rest," Anna said as she whipped up a large container of tuna salad and placed it in the refrigerator for tomorrow.

Anna and Chuck had moved to Ohio from the panhandle of Texas about ten years ago. Chuck's company had given him an ultimatum ... make the move or take any early retirement. Personally, I was extremely glad they had made the move. Anna was a true gem with her practical common sense and droll Texan humor. She had become like a family member to me. Her son, Stevie, had joined my cub scout den when he was younger and now our boys were inseparable and best friends. Thinking of Anna's family, an idea sprang to my mind.

"Why don't you guys come with us? I realize it's last minute but I can ask my mother-in-law if she knows of any other vacancies in the complex. It would be so exciting to tour the island together and the boys would certainly have a good time."

"What about the shop?" Anna asked with a wave of her hand.

"Let's close it for the week. We deserve a break and our bottom line won't suffer that much. Think of the operating expenses we'll save by being closed for a few days," I said with a laugh. "C'mon. Talk to Chuck about it and I'll call Maude."

"Wouldn't it be great if Colleen and Ron could join us? The guys could take off and fish all day while we girls explored the island," Anna suggested.

"You know, you've got a point. Most of those units contain three bedrooms. Doug mentioned that Harold and Maude would likely join us for a couple days. The condo we'll be in will be full—one bedroom for my boys and one for Doug and me plus his parents in the third. What if you and Colleen split the rent of a second condo, you'd each have your own bedroom with one left over for Stevie? As long as we can find a vacant unit, this might work."

"I really hope you find us a vacancy. It won't take much convincing to make Chuck pack his fishing gear and golf clubs."

Picking up my cell phone, I punched in Colleen's number and waited for her to pick up. My dear friend since grade school answered after the third ring.

"Hello?" Colleen's lyrical voice came through the line.

"Hey girl! What are you and Ron doing next week? Anna and I have a proposition for you," I said as I imagined her curiosity being piqued.

"What kind of proposition?" I could hear the wariness in her voice. "The last time I took you up on one of your propositions, I found myself hiding in a storage closet. So, although Ron and I have nothing

3

on the calendar for next week, I'm almost afraid to ask what you have in mind," Colleen said.

"Ye of little faith ... you wound me with your doubts," I chastised her in my best Shakespearean voice then laughed. "Seriously ... how would you and Ron like to join us up on Lake Erie for a week's vacation trip? Maybe team up with Anna and Chuck to split the cost of a condo? Doug's parents gave us the use of their rental unit on Put-in-Bay for next week."

Her squeal over the phone almost split my eardrum. "Really? You're going to be at the beach on an island for a week? Wow! Sounds like an ideal getaway. I'll ask Ron and call you back tonight. What type of costs are we looking at?"

"I'll have to let you know the details later. I'm going to phone my mother-in-law and see if she can help find another condo in the same complex so we can all be together."

"All right. I'll keep my fingers crossed and in the mean while, I'll speak to Ron. I don't expect any obstacles to prevent our going with you."

"Great! Talk with you later." I ended the call and smiled broadly at Anna. "Colleen and Ron are in. Now I just have to find you a rental."

"One we can afford," Anna reminded me.

We finished our closing routine and locked up the shop then I hurried home to call Maude Gardner. My mother-in-law and I aren't what you would call close, but she loves her grandsons and is more than generous with them, so I bide my sharp tongue. She tolerates me. I've always known she didn't approve of me marrying her son sixteen years ago, but hopefully she's gotten over it. Maude disapproved of our hasty marriage when I learned I was pregnant with our son Johnny. Because I quit school and only completed an associate's degree, she's looked down on me as being lower class. Whatever! Like I said, we tolerate each other in small doses. My desire to have my friends accompany me to Lake Erie next week was a purely defensive move ... less time spent in Maude's company and the safety of being surrounded by my buddies.

Stirring a pot of spaghetti sauce on the stovetop, I let my thoughts wander. Steam spiraled upwards from the large pot, adding to the summer heat. My mind proposed several strings of conversation with Maude as I prepared to phone her. Let's face it, I was procrastinating. Doug would be home soon. Maybe I could ask Doug to call his mother and ask about another vacant condo. His rapport with his mother was so much better than mine.

Just as I completed that thought, the kitchen door opened and in walked my knight in shining armor to save me from the dragon. I grinned as my husband entered the laundry room and went about taking off his gun belt and securing it in the gun cabinet, out of harm's way and young hands. Doug never failed to complete this routine safety procedure before joining the family. I nodded in approval and watched him as he walked to the kitchen sink to wash his hands. He looked so handsome in his uniform. I admit it; I was awfully proud of his recent promotion to sheriff.

He raised an eyebrow and shot me a look, no doubt wondering why my face wore such a silly expression.

"Do I want to know what you're up to?" he asked. He pressed a kiss to my cheek then surveyed dinner bubbling on the stove.

Our furry baby, an orange and white tabby cat named Mittens, interrupted us as he rubbed his back against my legs and butted me with his head, demanding my attention. I reached down and scratched his head but he wasn't satisfied with a mere token of affection.

"Mroww," Mittens whined his displeasure with me.

"I know you're hungry. Sorry you have to wait, but I hardly think you're starving to death," I told the cat.

I directed my attention back to my cooking, took a deep breath then took a roundabout approach to my dilemma.

"Hi honey, how was your day?" I asked as I turned toward Doug and filled a pot of water at the sink. Setting it on the stove to boil for noodles, I faced my husband. "I, um, mentioned our trip next week to Anna and Colleen. They'd like to come. What do you think?"

Doug swallowed a bite of garlic bread before answering. "Ron and Chuck coming too? Sounds like it would be a blast but where's everyone going to sleep?"

"Well of course, they would need to rent their own condo. I was sort of wondering if you'd call your mother and ask her if she knows of any other vacant rentals in her complex. If Anna and Colleen could share one of those three bedroom units, they'd have plenty of space and could afford it by splitting the cost. Would you mind calling her?"

"Mm-hmm, I get it. You don't want to speak to my mom." Doug sighed and ran his fingers through his dark hair. "All right, what am I supposed to ask her?"

"Maude's involved with the HOA in her complex. Maybe she can ask, or she might know already, if someone has an empty unit next week. Just ask her help in finding a place for our friends."

Doug grabbed a beer out of the refrigerator and took a healthy swig to fortify himself before he picked up his cell phone and dialed his parent's home number.

"You owe me, Meredith Gardner," he said with a wink as he waited for his call to be answered.

I answered him with an innocent smile of my own.

Chapter Two

Gift Horse

"I still can't believe it. This is going to be the best vacation trip ever," I said as I hugged Colleen. "You guys are getting a deal too. Maude told Doug she was overseeing the rental for one of the owners who traveled to Europe this summer. She's charging you half price of what that unit goes for in peak season. When you and Anna split that, you'll only have to pay six hundred for the entire week."

"The price is more than affordable. I've looked at staying on Put-in-Bay before but the costs were out of our reach. One last summer getaway before school resumes will be heaven," Colleen said as she reflected on returning to her duties as principal of the elementary school. She flicked her long auburn hair off her shoulders as we walked down the street toward Frannie's Frocks.

"Since it's the end of the season, Aunt Fran marked down her summer outfits. I'm eager to see what she has. I need to find something new to wear on the island."

My aunt, Frances Andrews, is both the owner of the cutest dress shop in town and, as of last summer, the recently elected mayor of our wonderful community.

Meadowood is a typical, small Midwestern town, home to families like mine who've resided here for generations — average, middle-income people that work for a living and support their community. We're within driving distance of several big cities and an hour away from the Ohio state capital, but we're still a rural community. Rolling hills, rich with flourishing farmlands, fill the countryside that surrounds our centuries-old town. Acres of corn and soybeans spread across the land like a lush green quilt, now awaiting the coming autumn harvest.

Stand still in the middle of Park Street and listen to the sounds of our small town. No loud annoying traffic noises—only friendly people chatting and greeting neighbors or happy kids on bicycles traversing the sidewalks, and a small volume of local cars driving slowly down the main streets. Meadowood is home, a community where folks feel safe, comfortable, and take pride in knowing all their fellow neighbors.

A tour of Meadowood makes you feel like you've stepped back in time. We celebrated our bicentennial last summer. Historic buildings and quaint store fronts line the principal thoroughfare through town. Large oak and maple trees border the streets and spread their canopies of leafy branches on each side. Ron Wythe's insurance office and Ted Williams's real estate sit side by side. A bakery and two banks, plus my aunt's dress shop, blend with various other retail businesses downtown. Our tea shop occupies a quaint cottage on the corner opposite Martha's bakery. All businesses inhabit brick or clapboard structures with peaked roofs, adorned by gables or dormers. Buildings date back over a hundred years. Not a single garish neon sign destroys the historic downtown image.

As we entered Frannie's Frocks, the bell above the door jingled and my aunt waved a greeting while she finished assisting her customer.

A widow, Fran was still an attractive woman with her dark blond hair streaked with a scattering of gray strands, the only sign of her advancing years. I've always thought I favored my aunt more than my mother since we have the same coloring ... both dark blonds with blue-gray eye color. The older I get, the more I think that's true, except I wear my blonde hair curly and short and Fran's is long. Although I wish I favored my aunt's figure instead of the full-figured curves I inherited from my mother. It's a constant battle keeping the expanding inches off my hips. We're both very close as niece and aunt. I swear at times she can read my mind. I love her dearly, plus I've got my aunt to thank for my share of the tea shop partnership since she generously invested in our venture a year ago.

Racks displayed lovely sweaters and fall dresses in the front of the store. Long sleeve polo shirts and corduroy pants lay in ready for brisk temperatures of the coming autumn season. I didn't want to contemplate the end of summer those clothes signified.

Colleen and I both zeroed in on the clearance display of summer shorts and tops in the back of the shop. Browsing through the folded pile of tops, I found an adorable nautical blue and white striped sleeveless top. I could just picture it worn with a pair of red or navy blue capris. Looking over at Colleen, I saw her eyes light up over a pretty pale-green eyelet cotton blouse. Green was Colleen's favorite choice with her Irish coloring. Let's face it, Colleen could wear burlap and still be beautiful ... my friend was a natural beauty with her peaches and cream complexion, emerald-green eyes, and flowing auburn hair.

"It was really nice of your mother-in-law to find us a place," Colleen commented as she sorted through a rack of dresses.

"Yes, it was. That's what's got me worried. I keep wondering what she's got up her sleeve. She's not normally so accommodating."

Aunt Fran heard my last comment and laughed. "Meredith Gardner, aren't you being rather harsh on Doug's mother? You should be grateful for her generosity."

Being duly chastised, I tried to look guilty but couldn't quite pull it off. "Jeez Louise—Aunt Fran, you've met the woman! Tell me you don't have the same suspicions as I do. It isn't in her character to be kind to me and you know it. I can't help but suspect an ulterior motive."

Fran chuckled and couldn't meet my eyes as she said, "Hmm, you've got a point. Still, take advantage of the gift horse while you can, even if it comes with a price tag later."

"Ha! You're not making me feel more confident."

"Who's taking care of Mittens while we're all at the lake?" asked Colleen.

"Who do you think?" Fran asked with a snort. "The fur ball will stay with me for the week, no doubt lounging on my sofa and leaving his hair all over the place."

"C'mon, you spoil him to death and will pamper him the entire week. Admit it ... you'll love having him there," I said as I placed an arm around my aunt's shoulder in a brief hug.

"I suppose he will keep me company when I get home from work," Fran admitted grudgingly, with a wink at Colleen.

"Have I told you how much I appreciate you?" I asked my aunt and planted a kiss on her cheek.

Loading the last suitcase into the back of our SUV, I reviewed my mental checklist and ticked off items in my head. Billy and Johnny had already climbed into the Santa Fe's back seat.

"I'll be right back," I said to no one in particular then dashed back into the house.

Walking around the kitchen, I unplugged the coffee maker, checked I had turned off all the burners on the stove, and made sure all the faucets were off in the bathrooms. Windows were locked and drapes drawn. I put lamps on timers and had watered the houseplants. Aunt Fran had collected Mittens and his belongings last night. Doug had turned the air conditioner on auto with a high setting that would keep it from running all the time while we were gone but would maintain a reasonable temperature in the house. Leaving the house empty for an entire week felt unsettling. We rarely left home more than a single night, let alone seven days.

"I'm turning off the main water valve. I don't want to come home to find the place flooded from a broken pipe," Doug said as he made his own inspections and precautions.

"All right. Good idea. I gave a key to Aunt Fran, just in case. Don't forget, you can always check the Ring camera on your phone to see what's going on. The boys are in the car. C'mon, let's go," I said as I pulled the back door closed.

Doug and I climbed into the car. We both looked over our shoulders at our sons. Doug insured seatbelts were in place while I glanced to make sure they had drinks and snacks for the trip. I still considered Billy and Johnny my little boys, forgetting the self-sufficient teenagers they'd grown into. I had the same feeling now in the pit of my tummy as when we drove the boys to summer camp a couple of years ago. Of course, the difference now was that we were going too. Doug backed out of the driveway and we were off. As we drove near Anna's house, they beeped their horn and pulled out to follow us up toward Port Clinton.

I could feel my excitement building as we drove. Gazing out the car window, farms and towns blurred as we sped up the highway heading north. The closer we got to Lake Erie, the more butterflies I felt. This was going to be a great adventure.

In two hours' time, we all met up at the Miller Ferry Service parking lot. We prepared to leave our cars for the week and board the ferryboat that would whisk us over to South Bass Island. The island was so small; the mayor prohibited cars except for year-round residents. Tourists used golf carts or bicycles to travel village streets and paths. Luckily, we had the use of our parent's golf cart at the condo, but Anna and Colleen each intended to rent a cart so the men and gals could split up occasionally.

We all parked our vehicles and unloaded the luggage; I had restricted each person to one bag and a carryon. Now our family joined the

Thompson's along with Ron and Colleen as we boarded the ferryboat for the twenty-minute sail to Put-in-Bay harbor.

The ferry ride was picture-perfect with bright blue skies and plenty of sunshine overhead instead of the usual gray Ohio clouds. Seagulls soared above; their cries carried on the stiff breeze. The boys, Billy and Johnny, leaned so far over the rail watching the wake of the boat, I thought they might fall in. Doug, ever the careful lawman and watchful father, kept a hand hovering near Billy's shirt collar just in case he had to pull him back. Billy was two years younger than his brother and could be a little scamp who often got into trouble.

My friends sat with other passengers under the protective canopy in the back of the boat. I waved to Colleen and Anna as I left my seat and set my sights on the scenery ahead.

The boat plowed through the white crests of Lake Erie. Navigating on wobbly sea legs, I stumbled a few times as I made my way toward the front of the boat. A seaman, dressed in the ferryboat's overalls, caught my arm and kept me from slipping on the wet deck as the boat dipped. I smiled and thanked the tall, older man with dark hair and a thin mustache. He nodded then braced his feet, efficiently coiling a line of rope, as Doug joined me near the bow.

Wind whipped the waves, spraying water off the boat's bow to mist my face and catch on my tongue. I felt disappointed there was no salty taste from the fresh water Lake Erie, unlike the ocean. It didn't seem right, somehow, a body of water so huge ... the Great Lakes resembled an ocean with waves and tides yet robbed of their salt. The air felt several degrees cooler as we approached the island, one of several dotting the Great Lake bordering the U.S. and Canada.

The island appeared like a dream: a cluster of colorful buildings nestled against rocky shores and sandy beaches, with the occasional bay laurel, ash, or oak trees towering above. It was a blend of charming and upscale—a place where you could lounge in flip-flops all day but still find a five-star meal at night.

As we neared the island, I spotted the tall Doric columns rising majestically of the Perry's Victory and International Peace Memorial monument that honored the Battle of Lake Erie from the War of 1812.

Pointing to the distant column, I drew the boy's attention to the historic monument. They nodded enthusiastically.

"We can plan on going there tomorrow if you want," I told my sons and Stevie.

Behind me, Doug stood with his hands on his hips, gazing at the shoreline with an expression I could only describe as suspicious. "It looks too quiet," he muttered, narrowing his eyes.

Holding onto the ship's railing, I turned to my husband, "Douglas Gardner! Really! You need to relax, Sheriff," I teased, bumping his arm with mine. "Promise me you'll try it this week. We're lucky Maude and Harold are giving us this break. We should do something nice to thank your parents."

Doug's lips twitched in a smile that he tried to hide, but I knew I'd scored a win. I tossed my head, shaking my unruly damp curls that clung to my forehead and cheeks.

The seaman's head jerked at mention of the Gardner name. His lower lip curled into a sneer before he averted his face, then made his way toward the stern to ready the gangway for disembarking.

The harbor occupied the southern side of the island. Sailboats, catamarans, and speed boats of all sizes sat moored within the protected marina. I spotted two impressive yachts tied to private docks whose ownership I could only imagine.

Once we docked and made our way off the ferry, the excitement ratcheted up another notch. The small village bustled with summer tourists, families on bikes, and golf carts zipping past. Quaint bed-and-breakfast inns dotted the streets leading from the marina. Intriguing shops and restaurants squeezed into the maze of avenues aching to be explored.

Luckily, the golf cart rentals were located close to the dock for the convenience of new arrivals with luggage in tow and needing transportation. Chuck and Ron each rented a cart. We hitched a ride with them, balancing our luggage on laps. We'd find our golf cart later housed within the condo carport.

The boys spotted a golf cart with outlandish flame decals parked nearby and immediately began debating how fast it could go.

"Probably not fast enough to outrun your dad," I said, laughing as Doug shot me a mock glare.

Anna turned back, her Texas twang warming her words. "Somehow I can't picture Doug on a red light run in one of those little toys. Don't imagine they travel faster than twenty-five miles per hour."

I laughed, imagining the image Anna described.

Doug spoke up and pointed his finger at me as we moved forward with a jolt on the electric cart. "Merry is the one with the lead foot. If anyone breaks the speed limit, it's her."

"Then these golf carts are going to be a unique experience for her," Anna commented.

"Hey! Who's side are you on?" I said with a laugh.

Checking my notes again, we made our way down the main street toward the high-rise condo unit three blocks inland. The path was narrow and climbed gradually up a hill. Rocky ledges fell away sharply to the lake below. Taking a deep breath, I smelled the spicy fragrance of bay laurel trees that bordered the path. We passed a local golf course and Chuck tooted his horn and waved to a pair of golfers ready to tee off.

Looking like a short caravan loaded to the brim, we continued to climb the incline and made our way to the rental office at the address Maude had provided. The guys parked our carts within the open carport next to the building.

I entered the office and greeted the man behind the counter. "Hello. I'm Meredith Gardner. My mother-in-law left a key to her condo for us. You should also have a key for our friends, the Thompsons and Wythes, who are renting the next door unit."

The attendant looked down at his ledger. "Yes. I spoke with Mrs. Gardner. Welcome to Put-in-Bay. I'm Maurice, at your service."

"Thank you." I held out my hand and he dropped in two keys on numbered rings.

"You're in unit two; your friends are in number four."

"Thanks again."

Stepping outside, I gazed up at the tall building.

It appeared our lodging for the week were condos on the top floor of the island's only high-rise. It wasn't the kind of place we were accustomed to—this building appeared sleek, modern, and with an infinity pool that gave the illusion it spilled directly into the lake below.

Anna and Chuck Thompson, with their son Stevie in tow, joined us near the building entrance. Anna, her usual vivacious self, whistled when she saw the building. "Merry, I thought you said this was just a little beach getaway. This looks like something out of a travel magazine."

"Nothing but the best for Maude. Couldn't imagine her staying in any place where she'd have to rough it. But don't worry," I said with a grin, "there's still sand. The boys will track it inside by dinner to make it look normal."

Ron and Colleen rolled their luggage toward the pair of elevators. The expressions of awe on their faces were priceless.

"Maybe we better divide up. I don't think we can all fit in one elevator with luggage. What floor are we on?" asked Colleen.

I glanced at the key in my hand. "Seventh. Billy and Johnny, you ride up with Mrs. Wythe." I handed Ron the key to their unit.

Doug and I piled into the elevator with Anna and family. We were cramped with luggage at our feet as we waited the few minutes it took for the elevator to rapidly rise to the top floor. The doors chimed as both elevators glided to smooth stops. We all stepped out into a wide carpeted hallway with four doors, two on each side of the hall leading into the residential units. Based upon the key numbers, our friends were staying in the condo directly next door to us.

Doug turned the key and we entered the apartment, then stopped in our tracks. Our eyes widened at the sight. The condo was stunning. Floor-to-ceiling windows offered a panoramic view of Lake Erie and the island below. Décor was all soft whites and calming blues, like floating on a cloud. The place oozed relaxation. The pristine kitchen with white cabinets and marble counters would pamper a gourmet chef.

Johnny and Billy dashed to claim their bedroom, and Doug let out a low whistle as he surveyed the space.

"Wow, this isn't bad," he admitted.

"Would you expect anything less for your mother? I bet Maude selected all the décor personally. This place definitely reflects her taste."

Walking down the short hall, I poked my head into the master bedroom reserved for my in-laws and the room claimed by the boys. They were already stuffing clothes into a chest of drawers and had turned on a TV. The third bedroom that Doug and I would occupy was roomy and nicely appointed, with a queen-size bed and more of the pale blue color scheme. It had a private bath that I appreciated and promised myself the enjoyment of a luxurious hot shower later. Smiling as I surveyed the room, I twirled around and stretched my arms above my head. This was going to be the best holiday ever!

"I'm dying to see what the girls' place looks like. I'll just be a minute. I'm popping next door. Be right back. Think about what you want to do first," I told Doug as I dashed next door and tapped on the door.

Anna opened the door, grabbed my hand, and pulled me inside. "Holy cow! Is this place for real? I feel like I need to take off my shoes and wash my hands before I touch anything. This is heaven!"

Colleen walked into the living room. She smiled from ear to ear. "Oh my gosh, I can't believe we're staying here for a week. I feel like I'm dreaming. This place is so elegant. Does your condo look as opulent as this one? What am I saying? It must. I know Doug's mother wouldn't settle for anything less."

I gazed about the plush room with its shades of beige and pearl white décor. The wall of windows provided a similar view like ours; off-white linen draperies framed the glass panels. Soft buttery tan leather sofas and pairs of matching chairs filled the living room. A wide-screen television covered one wall. The pristine kitchen included a packed pantry and refrigerator full of food choices.

"So you'll be comfortable staying here? You guys don't mind roughing it?" I laughed. Anna and Colleen both hugged me as we jumped up and down and giggled like schoolgirls.

"Let's get unpacked and check this place out," suggested Colleen. "I'm eager to explore the village and island."

Chapter Three

Parker

Closing the door to my friends' condo, I headed back to our own place but paused in the hall. I noticed one of the doors across from us was slightly ajar. Curiosity, ever my greatest weakness, got the better of me, and I wandered closer.

"Hello?" I called softly, peeking through the door opening. My eyes darted around the room. I immediately saw that this condo wasn't furnished as plush as our units. The furniture looked typical of a summer beach rental, serviceable and comfortable, but not expensive. No art décor graced the walls nor expensive window treatments, only vertical blinds stretched across the balcony doors.

A man stood just inside, adjusting what looked like a professional camera on a tripod. He turned at the sound of my voice, and his expression quickly shifted from surprise to guarded politeness. He moved toward me and the open door.

"Oh, sorry to bother you," I said quickly, holding up a hand. "I'm Meredith Gardner. My family just checked in across the hall."

"John Parker," he replied, stepping forward to shake my hand. He was in his late forties, with salt-and-pepper hair and a deep tan that only came from living near the beach year-round. "I'm staying here for a little ... work retreat."

"Photography?" I asked, gesturing to the camera.

He hesitated, just for a beat, before nodding. "Something like that."

"Nice! The views here are incredible. Are you shooting for a project?"

He gave a tight smile. "No, just a hobby."

Something in his tone that didn't quite match his words, but before I could press further, he stepped back into the condo and prepared to close his door. "Well, nice meeting you, Mrs. Gardner. Enjoy your stay."

"Thanks, you too," I said, although my curiosity was thoroughly whetted. There was something about the man that pricked my senses. I couldn't put my finger on it.

Walking back into our condo, I met Doug and the boys, all eager to go explore the village and island sights. Grabbing my purse, I slung the strap across my body and prepared for our first exploration. Pressing a kiss to my husband's cheek, I clasped his hand as we pulled the door behind us and met our friends at the elevator. I planned to let the mystery of Mr. Parker simmer for the evening since I had more pleasurable things to think about.

Deciding to walk the nearby streets, we left the golf carts parked for the time being as we got our bearings and scoped out the locale. Heat radiated from the pavements but a cool breeze blowing off the lake helped to dissipate it. It wasn't long belong before we broke off into three groups. The boys ran ahead to discover a miniature golf course that drew them in. I followed the girls into a cute souvenir shop filled with the sweetest sundresses and hats, plus a wide selection of Lake Erie decorated mugs, plates, and assorted objects stamped with the name or image of the island. Our husbands found a bait shop that offered fishing boat rentals that piqued their interest. Close to half an hour later, we all assembled on the sidewalk.

"I'm hungry," Billy complained.

"Me too," Stevie and Johnny both chimed in.

"Well, there's plenty of food back at the condo or we could find a place to eat while we're out," I said.

"No cooking on our first night here. Let's eat out," Doug commanded as he reached for my hand, swinging it as we strolled like a pair of teenagers.

"Hey, what about that place that boasts the longest bar in the world? Look at this brochure I picked up at the bait shop. See here ... Beer Barrel Saloon, should be about two blocks from here. What do you say? Let's give it a whirl," Chuck suggested.

"Chuck! A saloon ... really? What about the boys?" Anna gave him a mock punch in the shoulder.

"It'll be okay. C'mon, they've got burgers and hotdogs; the kids can drink soda. Bet you there'll be plenty of families in there," Chuck insisted.

With no other destination in mind, we agreed to walk the couple blocks to the Beer Barrel. We arrived to find lively music, laughter, and a tempting aroma spilling out of the restaurant where juicy burgers sizzled on the grill. One wall of the saloon was open to the street and views of the marina. A green and white striped canvas canopy extended overhead with stools tucked under the wide oaken bar that stretched the length of the street to the corner, then turned into the interior of the place. I shook my head at the sight; no wonder the saloon claimed the title of longest bar.

Chuck was right. Families of all ages filled the place. The noise level increased several decibels as we entered the door.

Looking around, we found a long picnic table inside that would accommodate all nine of us. A waiter handed us menus to study and left. My eyes widened at the numerous selections.

"Wow, they've got a lot to choose from. You guys want burgers and fries?" I asked Billy and Johnny. My sons and Stevie gave me an enthusiastic shake of their heads.

A few minutes later, the waiter returned to take orders for our group. I pointed to the boys and ordered the platter of hamburgers and fries, along with mugs of root beer.

"I'd like the fried shrimp basket with fries and a Coke," I said.

Doug pointed to a menu entry. "I'll have the grouper. Bring me a Bud light."

"That sounds good," Chuck said. "Bring me the same."

Colleen and Anna both ordered grilled white fish with baked potatoes and Ron asked for the double cheeseburger deluxe.

"Whoa, Ron! Did you see the size of that sandwich? Are you sure you're going to be able to eat that thing?" I asked.

"Mm-hmm, just watch me," Ron said with a wiggle of his eyebrows and a mischievous grin at Colleen.

We all laughed then our conversation became of blend of voices as we each expressed impressions of the island and the start of our vacation week.

"So what's on the agenda for tomorrow?" Anna asked.

Everyone turned to look at me. "Hey, I'm not the tour guide. Please feel free to explore on your own and do whatever interests you. I don't want anyone feeling obligated to do what I want."

"We're not. Just thought you might have some good ideas, that's all," Anna said as she took another bite of her dinner.

"Well ... I picked up a brochure about a winery tour. Sounds like fun. Doug's parents will arrive tomorrow morning. I was hoping Maude might stay with the boys later while we adults take the winery tour. The boys can swim in the pool or play some board games. I doubt Maude would be interested in touring the winery; she's probably been there dozens of times since she spends weeks on the island each summer. What do you think? We can relax at the pool in the early part of the day and check out the winery later."

"Sounds like a great plan. We can all sleep in, meet at the pool then enjoy the winery tour in late afternoon," Colleen agreed.

"Not all of us will get to sleep in," Doug reminded me. He pulled his face into a painful frown.

"Sorry dear, but they're your parents and we've got their golf cart. You'll have to drive down to the dock to pick them up tomorrow morning," I said with an innocent smile on my face, knowing I'd be avoiding contact with his mother for a bit longer.

As we finished our meal and the guys each took care of the bills, I experienced that prickly feeling on the back of my neck when something was wrong. I slowly turned around and scanned the room and the long bar. To my surprise, I spotted John Parker seated at a small table with his laptop open in front of him. Was he following us? Now why did I suddenly think that? Doug's paranoia must be rubbing off on me. He had every right to be in a public place like the Beer Barrel. Of course, it was simply a coincidence. That's all it was. Or was it? My mind couldn't accept that answer.

I pulled my compact out of my purse and pretended to powder my nose. As I held the compact, I turned my back on John Parker's table so I could capture him in my mirror. I watched as he casually lowered his head and focused on his computer screen. Tilting my mirror, I concentrated on the images reflected on his screen ... jeez Louise! Photographs of us were displayed on his laptop. Parker had taken pictures of Doug and me walking down the street. I recognized another one of Doug standing in the entrance to the bait shop. I couldn't make out the other pictures as Parker flipped through the images. How creepy! Why would he photograph us?

As soon as we strolled outside and I felt we were out of view and earshot, I pulled on Doug's arm and led him to a secluded spot behind an elderberry bush. I noticed Anna raised an eyebrow at my actions but stayed silent.

"What's wrong with you?" Doug asked in a loud stage whisper. He studied my face and realized I wasn't joking around.

"There's a man in that bar with photographs of us on his computer."

"What are you talking about? Pictures of us?"

"His name is John Parker. I met him at the condo earlier; he's across the hall from us. The guy is weird. He's a photographer or something. He had some expensive equipment in his living room with a camera on a tripod. Guess I assumed he was taking pictures of the island for a magazine spread, but I just recognized several shots of us on his laptop. That's too creepy for words. Why is this guy spying on us?"

"Are you sure what you saw? Maybe he was taking a picture of the street and we were simply in the background. I'm sure he captures other people in his shots; it's hard getting an empty frame, what with people walking everywhere," Doug reasoned.

"Maybe. But it didn't look like that and my prickly intuition says this is different. I'm gonna keep my eye on this dude," I said.

"Don't go sticking your nose into this man's business. We aren't in Meadowood. You get yourself in trouble here, I won't be able to get you out."

Doug drove to the wharf and picked up Harold and Maude as the ferry docked right on time the next morning. Luckily, Doug didn't have to haul any luggage since his parents kept a full wardrobe at the condo.

I hurried to make our bed and straighten up the condo before their arrival. Rushing into our bathroom, I dressed for the day in my new nautical top and navy capris then ran a comb through my short hair. Maude was a stickler for appearing stylish at all times. Greeting her at the door wearing my short baby doll pajamas and robe would never do. Vacation or not, a lady always looked presentable.

A pot of coffee perked on the counter, filling the kitchen with a rich aroma. A quick dash to the bakery down the street had provided a tray of delicious pastries, including cherry Danish and cream-filled donuts, to tempt the hungry diner. I arranged cups and small plates on the counter, to prepare a continental breakfast and coffee for the arriving travelers.

Billy and Johnny wandered into the kitchen; both boys wore their swim trunks, a t-shirt, and flip-flops.

"Your grandmother will be here any minute," I said.

"Do we have to stay? I just want a bowl of cereal and maybe one of those donuts with orange juice. We're gonna meet Stevie and get down to the pool," Johnny informed me.

"Yeah, Mom. We're on a mission," Billy told me with an emphatic nod of his head. Goggles that had been perched on his head slid forward with the movement and hung off his nose. He yanked them down.

"Grab your breakfast but you can't take off until you at least greet your grandmother and give her a kiss hello. Okay? Be polite while you're around her too. Remember, she's treating us to this week in her condo. So be nice."

"Okay, Mom. Don't worry. We'll be on our best behavior," Johnny promised me. A moment later, I heard the key in the lock and Doug ushered in his parents.

I pasted on my biggest smile and greeted them both.

"Did you have a pleasant crossing? I've got a continental breakfast ready for you but I can cook eggs if you'd prefer."

"Hello Meredith. I'm sure what you've fixed is lovely. Are you all settled in? What do you think of our little retreat?" asked Maude.

"It's perfect. Your choice of colors is beautiful. The condo is splendid with an amazing view. We couldn't be more comfortable. I wanted to thank you, too, for helping secure the unit next door for my friends. Their condo is wonderful."

"Fine. I'm glad they were satisfied. Douglas, take my carryon bag back to my room, please. Now, tell me what your plans are for today," Maude asked me in a convivial voice that I recognized more as a command. She poured a cup of coffee and served herself a fruit pastry.

I poured coffee for the rest of us, setting a mug down at Harold's place. Taking a couple eggs out of the refrigerator, I automatically started scrambling them and heated the frying pan for Doug's breakfast. My husband would require more than a donut to satisfy his morning hunger. I had his eggs cooking and ready to serve by the time he walked back into the kitchen.

"Thanks, Babe," Doug said as he slid onto a stool and reached for the pepper shaker. He took a sip of coffee and sighed appreciatively, then dove into his breakfast.

I noticed my mother-in-law nod in approval at my unspoken care of her son. After sixteen years of marriage, I think I knew what my husband liked in the morning! He didn't need to ask me, and I certainly didn't need any coaxing from his mother. But I was glad my actions had won me some brownie points with her.

After rinsing the pan in the sink, I took a sip of my coffee and bit off a piece of the cherry pastry. They were light and flaky, almost as good as the ones we bought for our tea shop from Martha's bakery.

"Mmm, these are yummy." Answering her previous question, I said, "Everyone wanted to enjoy the pool and relax in the sunshine today. Later, I wondered if you'd mind staying home with the boys while we visited the Harriman Winery. I understand they give a tour with wine tasting. It isn't something the boys would enjoy at their age," I said.

"Of course, Harold and I will keep an eye on them. I've taken that vineyard tour before; you'll like it."

"Thank you. Perhaps tomorrow we can all attend one of the outdoor concerts. I read a flyer advertising a concert of big band music being performed in the amphitheater."

"Really? Yes, that sounds marvelous. It will do the boys good to hear some decent orchestral music instead of that racket played on the radio nowadays."

I hid a grin behind my coffee cup. The boys better be on their best behavior today or knowing my mother-in-law, they'll be receiving lessons in proper manners. And she was correct; as always, they would benefit from listening to an orchestral concert.

Chapter Four

Winery

My nose itched slightly from a touch of sunburn. I preached at the boys to use sunscreen then didn't take my own advice while we spent the morning around the pool. In my defense, I did apply the lotion to arms and legs but had forgotten to dab it on my face. The salt water pool felt like bath water; the temperature warmed by the sun. The boys dived in and splashed around until the men joined them and challenged them to a game of water volley ball.

"Go Ron! Show them how it's done!" Colleen cheered on her husband as she lounged on the chaise.

Anna and I clapped and laughed as our sons trounced their fathers. Finally Chuck pleaded a leg cramp to give him an excuse to climb out of the pool and stretch out on a chaise lounge. Doug and Ron followed him seconds later.

It was the perfect start to a fun vacation experience for our families. Yes ... this was going to be the best vacation.

Enjoying the first adult-only activity of our vacation, South Bass Island was everything I'd hoped it would be. The approaching sunset was that perfect golden-pink that only seems to happen over water. We'd booked a tour of the local winery, a place called Harriman Vineyards that boasted "views you'll die for," according to the brochure. I should've taken that as a warning.

Doug, ever the stoic lawman, was less impressed by the setting than I was. "Just a winery," he said as we pulled up. "They're all the same—grapes and glasses." But I knew he'd secretly wanted a little downtime as much as I did. His cases back home had taken a toll on him, and a week on the island, away from Meadowood and its ever-demanding issues, sounded like the ideal escape for him. Even his parents appeared more relaxed, less stuffy, on the island.

I think my friends felt the same, as I glanced over at Ron and Colleen holding hands like newlyweds. Anna and Chuck appeared relaxed and whispered to each other like lovers. The island had spun its magical, romantic web to snare us all.

We joined the small gathering of tourists as we slowly strolled the vineyard grounds. We walked between the carefully tended arbors. The scents of rich soil and grapes blended into an earthy perfume.

Acres of grape vines filled rows upon rows in the vineyard. It was difficult to imagine the quantity of land devoted to the winery on an island of limited size. The deep purple-blue merlot grapes hid among the wide green leaves clinging to the arbors. Their large berries created the wine's rich flavor profile that Harriman's was known for: including blackberry, plum, cherry, chocolate, and spicy notes.

Our guide, Joe, mid-thirties, all sunburned cheeks and enthusiastic grins, led us and a handful of other tourists across the grounds. Joe was a friendly guy you couldn't help but like, with a knack for telling a story that made even Doug crack a smile.

The winery building was a historic stone structure with ivy vines creeping up its sides, giving it an old-world charm that could've been right out of Europe. Our guide led us into the cellar ... a dim, cool space almost cave-like, that smelled faintly of oak and yeast fermentation.

"This is where the magic happens, folks," he said, gesturing grandly around the room. "The Harriman family's been making wine here for four generations. The soil here on the island is something special."

"Doesn't it get too cold on Lake Erie?" asked one of the visitors.

"Special smudge pots and tarps protect our vineyard in winter months plus the cellar caves hold our vats."

The group listened attentively as Joe continued. Doug stood close by with his arms crossed. I nudged him, whispering, "Relax, Sheriff. Not every cellar hides a skeleton."

He smirked. "Wanna bet?"

I chuckled, but the deeper we moved into the cellar, the more the atmosphere made me feel odd. A faint smell wafted through the space, barely noticeable over the tang of the barrels. At first, I thought I smelled the peculiar scent of old wood, damp from the cool cellar air. But it was strangely acrid, woodsy, rather like absinthe or expensive truffles. I shrugged it off, chalking it up to my imagination.

As we moved back through the tasting room, Doug's hand held mine and I felt a reassuring comfort. We didn't often get to appreciate each other's companionship and partake in adult-only outings. Today, with the kids back at the condo with their grandparents, we could just enjoy behaving like other couples.

The tasting room contained a polished oaken bar with a handful of bistro tables and chairs scattered around the room. Wine racks filled the wall behind the bar and open shelves held a collection of wine glasses and other stemware. The tiled slate floor radiated cold under my sandals' thin soles, capturing the chilly temperatures of the cellar below. A bartender served small glasses of wine. We each sipped the sampling of wines, noting its bouquet and color as instructed, then received a fresh glass of the next vintage.

"This place is amazing," Colleen said as she and Ron sipped their wine samples. Their gaiety was contagious.

"Makes me think of Napa, California. Chuck and I once visited some vineyards when we spent a week in San Francisco. Some of those wineries store their casks in caves too," Anna told us as she held her glass up to the light to inspect the wine.

The quiet bartender poured more samples for tasting and slid them forward across the varnished oak surface. I took mine and slid the other glass toward Doug. Seeing Joe step toward us, Doug slid his glass toward Joe and took the next one.

Joe stood in front of the gathered visitors and held the wine glass up to the light. Bringing our attention to the merlot's clarity, the deep red hue sparkled under the glowing lights. He took an appreciative sip and talked about the age of the grapes and the length of time fermentation required.

In the middle of Joe's explanation of the vineyard's prized merlot, his face suddenly went white as a sheet. He stumbled, gripping the edge of the tasting counter.

"Sorry, folks," he murmured, sounding almost embarrassed. "Not sure why ... oddly bitter ..." He wiped his forehead, but his hand shook, and in a split second, his legs buckled.

"Joe?" a woman called out.

I jumped forward instinctively, but Doug was faster, catching Joe as he slumped to the ground.

"Everyone back!" Doug barked, his lawman's voice cutting through the sudden panic.

He kneeled beside Joe, feeling for a pulse. I hovered at Doug's shoulder, one eye on Joe's face. He looked strange. His skin had become grayish, and his eyes, when they opened briefly, were unfocused and glassy.

I leaned close, smelling that acrid, woodsy tang again. "Doug," I whispered. "Do you smell that?"

He looked up, just as concerned as I was. "Yeah. It's almost like ... truffles. Wolfsbane smells like that."

A horrible suspicion flickered to life in my mind, but I pushed it away. It couldn't be that. This was supposed to be a winery tour, not one of Doug's crime scenes. But the metallic scent, Joe's strange symptoms ... I couldn't shake the prickly feeling that something was terribly wrong.

By now, Joe's breathing was labored and irregular. Doug had his phone out, calling for an ambulance, his tone brisk and professional. I wanted to scream that this wasn't happening, that Joe was just dehydrated or maybe had a touch of food poisoning. But then he gasped, his eyes rolled back, and just like that, he was gone.

The EMTs arrived not long after, but clearly, there wasn't much they could do. Doug and I stood back with our friends. The small crowd of tourists gathered in shocked silence. I looked at Doug, and he looked back at me, a silent agreement passing between us. This was no accident.

The local Put-in-Bay police spoke to the paramedics and glanced toward where Doug and I stood. I could tell by the silent conference that they must have asked who reported it.

Minutes later, I was right. One of the policemen, wearing sergeant stripes on his sleeve, approached Doug. He appeared to be in his late twenties, freshly shaven, and extremely nervous.

"You Gardner?" asked the sergeant. "Understand you phoned it in. Can you tell me what happened?"

Doug spoke in a low voice, pointing to our group and the dead guide. "We had finished the tour of the vineyards and begun the tasting ... maybe about four samples at that point. Spent about twenty minutes in the tasting room. Joe took a sip of the merlot wine sample then faltered and looked ill. He slumped over. I noticed a gray pallor to his skin, shallow respirations, and a faint bitter odor."

"Thanks. That's a lot of keen detail. If you don't mind my asking, what do you do for a living, Mr. Gardner?"

"I'm the sheriff of Meadowood in Knox County."

"Say listen," the policeman drew Doug off to the side, where he could speak privately. In a low tone, he began again, "I've only got two officers working with me in the village. Mostly we give out parking tickets and oversee drunks in the local bars. This thing ... suspected murder ... it's out of our league. Would you mind helping out? I mean, advise me on what to do."

"You understand I'm out of my jurisdiction. Why don't you call in the state police? Don't they oversee the islands?" Doug inquired.

"State police are over in Sandusky. I'd, uh, kind of like to handle this locally, if we can. Would mean a real feather in my cap. Maybe a promotion that would get me off this island and a chance to join a bigger police force. So, what do you say? Can you give me some pointers?"

Doug glanced back at me. I could see him shift his shoulders as he adjusted his stance. I knew that look.

"What's your name sergeant? Give me a phone number where I can reach you." Doug tapped in the policeman's information on his cell phone then shared his phone number with the younger man. "I'll call your office tomorrow. I've got to see my wife and friends safely back to our condo."

"Okay. Thanks."

"In the meanwhile, you better collect those glasses for testing, dust for fingerprints, and take statements from everyone in attendance. Have the doctor run a toxicology report for poison," Doug suggested to the young officer.

A woman from the winery staff ushered us all back to the main building. Joe's last words hung in the air. His life cut short ... just like that. But why? And who would have done it? And now it appears Doug would be involved in the case. That was probably the only thing that didn't surprise me.

Chapter Five

Runaway Danger

As we drove back to the condo high-rise, Doug was unusually quiet. I could tell he was running through his mental checklist, putting pieces together even though he technically was off duty. I wanted to ask him what he thought, but I wasn't sure I wanted to hear the answer.

That night, a subdued Colleen, Ron, Chuck, and Anna returned to their condo to settle in and watch a movie. Doug and I sat on our balcony, listening to the waves lap against the shore. I could see the worry lines creasing his forehead, the same ones that showed up whenever he was deep into a case.

"Merry," he finally said, his voice low, "that smell—it was poison."

I felt a chill run through me. "You think someone deliberately killed Joe?"

Doug looked out over the water, his jaw tight. "I don't know. But the way he reacted, the symptoms ... it fits." He hesitated, his eyes flickering with something I couldn't quite place. "But what if ... what if it wasn't meant for him?"

My stomach dropped. "Doug, what are you saying?"

He looked at me, a haunted expression in his eyes. "What if that poison was meant for me?"

"How could it be meant for you?" I asked.

"When the bartender poured the wine for tasting ... he pushed a glass toward me, but I passed it along to the guide and took the next one. That poison should have been in my glass."

I wanted to laugh it off, tell him he was just being paranoid. But deep down, I knew he could be right. The idea settled over me like a storm cloud, dark and heavy. Doug had arrested his share of criminals over the years. Some of them held grudges that went beyond prison walls.

"So what now?" I asked, struggling to keep my voice steady. "You think someone followed us here? To an island in the middle of Lake Erie?"

He shrugged, but his shoulders were tense. "It wouldn't be the first time someone tried to get back at me. But here? That's what bothers me."

"What about that guy, John Parker? He acted suspicious when I met him and then those pictures he had on his computer—could he be tracking you? Was he at the winery? Did you see him?"

"No, I don't think so, but then I wasn't looking either."

The next day, I couldn't shake the feeling of being watched. I pulled the draperies closed, blocking the living room view, and kept our bedroom windows covered as well. Doug phoned Sergeant Drake shortly after he got up then drove to the station to consult with him before the family got out of bed.

I questioned him when he returned an hour later. "Well, what's the verdict?"

"Nothing official yet. The town doctor is examining the body. This place doesn't have a coroner so Drake has to wait on the doctor's medical report for any confirmation of poison. He probably won't know until tomorrow, but you saw what I did. Not much doubt, our guide was poisoned. I gave the sergeant some pointers on what procedures to take next. That's all I can do for the time being."

"Okay. I don't think we should tell the others about your suspicions. I don't want the boys worried, or your parents."

"Agreed. Let's go about our day as intended."

We had promised the boys a driving tour of the island ending at the monument. Our friends took off for separate destinations but would meet later for dinner. Doug left me the golf cart and walked the four blocks into town to buy concert tickets for all of us. I told him I'd meet him with the golf cart so we could start our tour and explore Perry's monument. Johnny and Billy were eager to climb the enormous tower.

Using my in-laws' golf cart was a fun, easy way to get around the island. The kids loved riding on it, and even I had to admit it made a charming way to get around—until I felt the brakes go out.

We were heading downhill from the condo toward town. I pressed the brake pedal instinctively, only to feel it sink uselessly under my foot. Panic shot through me as I gripped the wheel tighter. The boys were in the back, laughing, oblivious to the danger. Pulling up on the emergency brake made no effect. I hung onto the wheel of the cart, sniffing the faint, unfamiliar smell of burning rubber.

"Help!" I yelled into the air, but my voice was lost on the breeze. The cart accelerated, careening down the hillside path.

"Mom, why are we going so fast?" Billy asked. His eyes grew wide as the cart gained more speed.

"Hold tight!" I shouted to the boys.

My heart raced as I attempted to steer the runaway vehicle. The speed made the cart buck and jerk. It went faster with each second. Ahead, the narrow road twisted sharply, leading down toward a cliff with only a low wooden fence at the edge. I gritted my teeth, a death grip on the wheel, and tried desperately to think of a way out.

Up ahead, I saw Doug approaching on foot. He spotted our runaway cart. His eyes widened when he realized what was happening. In an instant, he broke into a sprint, running full out like a track star. Doug leaped forward to grab the cart's side as we hurtled toward him. Straining, he hauled himself up into the front seat next to me.

"Doug, the brakes—they're gone!" I gasped, my voice thick with fear. Our eyes met, understanding the danger all too well.

"Hang on!" He shouted, grabbing the wheel.

Together, we steered the runaway cart, but the cliff loomed closer. With a last-ditch maneuver, Doug threw his weight to the right side, jerking the wheel to veer the cart off the path, away from the looming cliff edge. The golf cart plowed into the ninth hole of a local golf course as Doug forced the runaway vehicle toward the golfers' deep sand trap, where it shuddered to a stop.

For a moment, silence settled over us, broken only by the waves' roar below and the low whimper of the boys clinging onto the back seat, afraid for their lives. We hugged each other in relief. Doug and I exchanged a look of gratitude and determination—the accident confirmed someone was out to harm us.

"Are you both okay?" I asked as I reached for my son's hands, relieved when they mutely nodded.

Doug balled his fists and punched the dashboard. He swore a few curse words under his breath. Through clenched teeth he growled, "No one puts my family in danger. I promise you honey, I won't stop until I find who's behind this."

"I don't understand ... first the winery and now the golf cart. That cart was okay yesterday and earlier when you used it. How can anyone know what our plans are or where we'll be? I have to admit, I'm scared. The boys and I almost crashed over a cliff!"

"Unfortunately, those carts sit under an open carport roof. They're protected from weather but open to anyone in the building to tamper with. There's no lock, only the key to the motor. The brake line's definitely been cut. I'm calling the village police and reporting this incident. I don't want you going anywhere without me. Okay?" Doug asked.

I nodded my agreement but couldn't help worrying. Our friends needed to be warned, too. What if one of them became injured while being in our presence? I'd never forgive myself. It wasn't fair to make them unwitting targets.

The quaint streets of Put-in-Bay no longer felt welcoming. Each friendly face now seemed like it hid something sinister. I intended to keep my boys close. Doug was visibly on edge. His eyes constantly scanned our surroundings and strangers nearby.

He stared into the distance while he ran his fingers through his hair. I knew he had strained to search his memory of past threats or cases with disgruntled perpetrators that might be behind this. Like looking for a needle in a haystack.

Doug made his call into the police station and explained the situation to the young policeman. I watched his face as he spoke and recognized the volcano of anger simmering beneath the surface.

Sergeant Drake had our golf cart towed from the golf course into a local garage. We told his parents that the cart needed new brakes and left it at that. The mechanic promised the cart would be repaired and returned by the next day. An easy fix ... if only my emotional despair could be resolved as easily.

I felt like we had a target on our backs, and it scared me. I'd been in tough scrapes in the past, mostly of my own making, but this time it seemed different. This time, the killer put my sons at risk. Nobody messes with my family ... not if they knew what was good for them. When my children were threatened, I became a fierce mama bear that would fight until my last breath.

Chapter Six

Imposter

The near crash of the golf cart still had my heart thumping and my blood boiling as I climbed into the squad car with Sergeant Drake. Merry and the boys were safe—thank God—but I couldn't shake the feeling that the universe was throwing bricks at me to get my attention. Poison at the winery, the brakes on the golf cart tampered with, and now I found myself roped into investigating a death that wasn't meant to happen.

Sergeant Drake drove the island's only police cruiser as we headed back to Harriman Winery. A murder had happened on my watch, on my supposed vacation, and I couldn't shake the sense that someone wanted it to be me instead of the poor tour guide.

Drake gripped the wheel like it might run off on its own. He was young—couldn't have been over 25—and had that eager, slightly nervous energy of someone still getting used to a badge. His uniform was neat, and he was trying hard to exude confidence, but the way he glanced at me every few seconds made it clear he was leaning on me for guidance.

Drake studied me as we pulled out of the condo parking lot. "Um, Sheriff Gardner, how's your wife holding up? And the kids?"

"You can call me Doug. They're shaken, but Merry's tougher than she looks. She's already trying to connect the dots. Merry can be quite the sleuth, despite my warnings."

"She always like that?"

"Always," I said, with equal parts pride and exasperation. "But this time, I can't blame her. That poison was meant for me."

Drake let out a low whistle. "Sheriff Gardner," he said, his voice cracking just slightly before he cleared his throat. "Uh, I mean, Doug. Do you really think they intended that poison for you?"

I leaned back in the seat, my gaze on the island's peaceful streets as we passed. "It fits. The victim wasn't supposed to take my glass. Whoever did this had a target in mind, and it wasn't Joe. I've been a cop long enough to know when someone's gunning for me."

Drake nodded, his jaw tightening. "I've never dealt with anything like this before. We usually get golf cart thefts and drunk tourists, not ... murder."

I gave him a sideways glance, softening my voice. "That's a good thing, Sergeant. You don't want too much experience with this kind of mess."

He gave a nervous chuckle. "Guess you've handled plenty of it, though."

"More than I'd like," I admitted. "The longer you wear the badge, the more you realize not everyone you put away will let it go. I've had my share of close calls. And now it looks like this one followed me here."

We pulled up to Harriman Winery just as the last hints of twilight faded into night. The tasting room glowed invitingly, but the energy inside was different now—subdued, wary. A few patrons lingered over glasses of wine, but the staff wore tense expressions. Whispers and side glances replaced the usual buzz of a lively winery filled with tourists.

Drake held the door for me, and I stepped inside, scanning the room. The bartender was wiping down the counter—a young woman with auburn hair tied in a bun. She didn't match the man who had served me yesterday.

"That's not him," I murmured to Drake, and he blinked in surprise.

"Not who?"

"The bartender who served me the poisoned wine. This isn't the same person."

Drake grimaced, looking uneasy. "Maybe there was a shift or scheduling change?"

"Let's find out." I approached the bar, keeping my movements calm and deliberate. "Excuse me. I'm Sheriff Doug Gardner, here with Sergeant Drake. Can we ask you a few questions?" I pulled out my I.D. card and motioned to the sergeant in uniform.

The bartender—her name tag read *Emily*—stopped mid-polish and nodded. "Of course, Sheriff. How can I help?"

"You weren't working yesterday, were you?" I asked.

She glanced between us, a frown wrinkled her brow. "Yes, sir; I was here. I came on at four," she said, glancing at Drake nervously. "Is this about what happened to our tour guide?"

"It is," I said, keeping my tone steady. "The person behind the bar yesterday—tall man, dark hair, thin mustache, maybe mid-forties. Who was he?"

Emily's eyes widened. "I'm sorry, sir, but there's no one here who matches that description. I'm the only bartender scheduled. If I'm not here then our owner, Mary Harriman, serves the early tour groups."

Drake and I exchanged a look.

"Are you sure?" I pressed. "I spoke to him directly. He poured my glass himself."

Emily shook her head, looking genuinely confused. "I don't know what to tell you. We don't have anyone like that on staff."

My stomach sank, the pieces clicking into place. "Then whoever was behind the bar wasn't supposed to be there."

Drake's eyes widened. "You mean ... an impostor?"

"Looks that way," I said grimly.

Emily, now visibly distressed, stammered, "I-I'm so sorry, Sheriff. I had no idea. If someone was pretending to work here, I didn't see him. I was on duty all evening; I only stepped away once to retrieve more bottles from our wine cellar."

"It's not your fault," I said, softening my tone. "But if you think of anything unusual—someone hanging around, acting suspicious—or someone who looks like the man I described, let us know." Drake handed the woman his business card.

She nodded, and we stepped back, moving to the quieter corner of the room.

Drake broke the silence first. "This is way out of my league, Doug. You're saying this guy faked his way into a job just to target you?"

"That's exactly what I'm saying," I replied. "And it wouldn't be the first time someone's tried something like this. A few years back, I put away a man running a drug ring out of his family's business. His brother came after me with a Molotov cocktail. Another time, I busted a guy for fraud who sent letters threatening to take out my family. This job doesn't leave you many friends, Drake. Some of them don't forget."

Drake ran a hand through his hair, his nervous energy practically buzzing. "But why here? Why now?"

"Maybe because I'm off-duty," I said simply. "He thought I'd have my guard down. That I wouldn't see it coming. I don't know ... maybe it was a spur of the moment decision on his part and he simply took the opportunity."

Drake shook his head. "This is insane. Do you think the guide was just ... wrong place, wrong time?"

"Exactly," I said, the weight of it settling heavily on my chest. "He wasn't supposed to die. The poor guy drank poison intended for me. An innocent man died because of me."

I dragged my hand through my hair and turned to the young policeman. "I tell you Drake, that's too many close calls. Someone wants me gone. The guide's death was an accident, then a sloppy second attempt with the golf cart. Who's next is the real question?"

Drake frowned. "If it's this personal, Doug, you might be safer heading home. Let me handle this."

"Not a chance," I said. "They came after my family, Drake. I'm staying until I figure out who's pulling the strings. And I'm not letting them get another shot."

Drake swallowed hard, his expression somewhere between disbelief and determination. "So what now?"

"We find the impostor," I said firmly. "He's our best lead. Someone wanted me dead, and this guy's either the trigger or the middleman. Either way, he's guilty and I want him."

Drake nodded, his nervousness giving way to resolve. "I'll pull any footage we can find from the winery cameras and get statements from the rest of the staff."

"Good," I said. "And while you do that, I'm going to make sure my family stays safe. Whoever this is, they already tried twice. They won't stop now."

Drake gave a sharp nod and headed off to make calls, leaving me standing in the darkened vineyard. The vines rustled softly in the breeze, and I couldn't help but feel like I was being watched.

This wasn't over. Not by a long shot. And the more I thought about it, the clearer it became: the bartender hadn't just been serving wine. He'd been serving a message. And now it was up to me to figure out who sent it—and stop them before they tried again. Maybe it was time for a family counsel, time to confide what was going on before anyone else was harmed.

Chapter Seven

Pow-Wow

We had agreed to meet in Maude's apartment before leaving for the afternoon concert. I'd sent Colleen and Anna text messages asking them to come over; it was important. Now Doug and I took turns pacing the living room floor as our friends and family sat gathered around, curious about what was so important. Anna and Chuck had taken the armchairs. My tea shop partner knew me well enough to watch and listen. Anna's expression was one of speculation. Colleen and Ron sat shoulder to shoulder, his arm protectively around her shoulders. Both appeared puzzled but patient. One glance at Maude and Harold perched on bar stools confirmed their irritation at being mandatorily summoned to a conference.

"Before we leave for the concert, there's something you need to know. Let me start by saying, I'm sorry I've put all of you in this situation. I didn't mean to ruin your vacations," Doug said. He dragged his fingers through his hair like he always did in times of aggravation or deep thought.

"What situation are you talking about?" asked Ron.

"The guide who died at the winery ... Joe? He was poisoned. The glass of wine that he drank should have been mine. Someone tried to kill me but an innocent man died instead," Doug said. He paced in front of us again, stopping to study the group before him.

You could have registered the level of shock on everyone's faces with a Richter scale. All three of the boys sat silently, in the same way as when they watched a horror movie that scared them but still couldn't look away. Glancing over at my mother-in-law, I thought she was about to faint. I hurried into the kitchen for a glass of water and pressed it into her hand.

"Drink this," I told her. She raised her eyes to me and nodded as she slowly took a sip.

"Are you sure, Doug?" asked Chuck.

"Yes, I'm afraid so. The local police have asked my help to investigate. We spoke to the staff at the winery and it seems the man who served us was not one of their employees. The guy was an imposter who saw a chance and took it. I don't know who he is or why he's seeking revenge."

I stepped forward and laid my hand on my husband's arm as I faced our friends and family.

"Yesterday, I had a near crash on the golf cart when I drove toward town. The boys can tell you ... it was frightening. The brake line had been cut and we barreled down the path toward the cliff. We would have gone over too, if Doug hadn't jumped onboard and steered us into a sand trap on the golf course," I said. Dead silence filled the room from my stunned audience then everyone began speaking at once.

"Oh my goodness!" exclaimed Colleen.

"Whoa! Like a runaway stagecoach," Anna declared.

"My poor babies!" Maude cried as she wrapped her arms around Billy and Johnny in a smothering hug.

Johnny rolled his eyes and Billy's face contorted under his grandmother's sudden exuberant affection.

"So that's why the cart is in the garage. Did Charlie say he could repair the brake line?" asked Harold in a calm voice.

"Yeah, Dad. The mechanic is installing a new line. Should be ready to pick up later this morning." Doug held up his hands to silence all the murmurs. "The thing is, Merry and I thought you should all know what's going on and be on alert. The last thing we want is to put anyone in danger simply by being in our company. We'll understand if you feel safer by leaving for home. I promised I'd stay on the island to assist the local cops. Plus, I admit, I want this guy who killed the tour guide and put my family at risk. He's not going to stop until he's either caught or is successful," Doug said in a taut voice. He slowly clenched and unclenched his fists to diffuse his anger.

Anna was the first to speak up. She and Chuck exchanged a silent agreement in that way married couples often do when no words were needed. "We're staying! I paid good money for that condo and we're going to enjoy the rest of our vacation week. There's safety in numbers. Isn't that what they always say? Well, I say we stick together and work together to figure this out," Anna stated defiantly in a show of her Texan grit.

"I agree. If we were back home, what would we all be doing? More than likely, Merry would be roping us into snooping around to solve the mystery. Okay, so let's do that here. Just because we aren't home doesn't mean we aren't all together. I say ... we're a team," Colleen said. She and Ron clasped hands and both nodded in agreement as they looked about the room.

"Are you sure? I don't have the same resources here. Maybe if we all stick together, like you said, we'll be safer," Doug said.

"Where do we start?" asked Harold.

"Guess the first thing we need to do is pick up your golf cart from Charlie. Can you call him and ask if it's ready? I'll walk down and pick it up."

"No need to walk, I'll give you a lift with our cart," Chuck suggested.

"Okay. Thanks. Once we all have our rides, let's go out to Perry's Monument like we promised the boys and then attend the concert at four o'clock. I'll give Drake a call and see if he has anything new to go on," Doug said.

Everyone rose and moved about; the boys scooted back to their bedroom to play video games until it was time to leave. Anna and Colleen sidled next to me, concern etched on their faces.

"Why didn't you tell us about the near crash yesterday? Oh my gosh, I can't even imagine how scary that was for you," Colleen whispered to me.

"I'm sorry. Doug didn't want to worry anybody until he knew what had happened," I said as I motioned them to follow me onto the balcony.

"I know that look," Anna said as we stepped onto the balcony and slid the door closed. "What do you have percolating in that devious mind of yours?"

"The day we arrived, I had left your apartment when I noticed the door across the hall standing ajar. Naturally I peeked inside and met the guy staying there."

"Naturally," Anna said with a snort. I shot her a look then continued my story.

"He's a photographer; at least that's what I thought because of all the cameras and tripods he had set up."

"Okay. So you met our neighbor. What's his name?" asked Colleen.

"John Parker. But here's the thing ... I saw him again at the Beer Barrel Saloon when we were there. He had his laptop with him and I spotted pictures of us on his screen. Isn't that weird? I think he's spying on us. Maybe he's the one who sabotaged our golf cart. What do you think?"

"Hmm, I think we should pay a neighborly visit to Mr. Parker. I sure 'nuff don't like somebody taking pictures of me and my kid without my knowing," Anna drawled. Her ire building.

"I was hoping you'd say that. We just need to plan when would be the right time to confront him," I said.

The sliding glass door glided open and Maude stepped out onto the balcony.

"What are you gals plotting out here? I hope you aren't planning something foolish, Meredith," Maude said as she cast an accusing eye on each of us.

"We were just discussing your neighbor, John Parker," I answered her.

"Who? There's no one else on this floor, at least not this month. Elsa Monroe lives across from your unit," she said, pointing to Anna and Colleen, "but she's in Europe this month. The other unit is empty while it's being renovated."

"Wait a minute. I met a guy living in the condo right across from us. He's a photographer and told me his name was John Parker. I was just telling the girls that I caught him taking pictures of us. Creepy. Jeez Louise, you mean he shouldn't be there?" I asked my mother-in-law. Wow, Mr. Parker became more and more suspicious.

"Certainly not. I'm the HOA secretary; I'm aware of everyone renting or owning units in this building. Well ... I'll just see about this so-called John Parker and find out what he's doing in that apartment," Maude stated with a look of determination on her face and fire in her eyes. She slid the door open and marched into the living room, grabbed a ring of keys off the counter, and headed for the front door.

Uh-oh, I think I just kicked over a hornet's nest. Doug would not like his mother storming into a suspect's apartment, especially if the man might be a murderer. I glanced at Anna and Colleen and we all rushed to squeeze through the open doorway to follow my crusading mother-in-law.

"Which unit did you see this Parker fellow occupying?" demanded Maude as we stood in the center of the hallway.

I pointed to the door opposite us.

"Hmph!" Maude pounded on the door. The sound reverberated loud enough to wake the dead. We waited. When no one opened the door, I watched my mother-in-law sort through a ring of keys then insert one into the lock.

Anna and Colleen both gasped. I gently pressed my hand onto Maude's as she reached for the doorknob.

"Don't you think we should call Doug? Do you really intend to bust into the apartment? Won't you be trespassing or something?"

"Let go of my hand. I'm perfectly within my rights to inspect this unit. You don't seem to realize that I'm responsible for these condos as the HOA secretary while the owners are gone. If you say there is a man staying in here, then I need to know. I'm going inside. You can come along or not," Maude stated emphatically.

There was no hesitancy on my mother-in-law's face, only righteous anger. My opinion of her raised a notch. I smiled at her fearless attitude.

"I'm coming, of course. I wouldn't let you face that man alone," I said.

"All right then." A slight smile curved her lips as she nodded her head. Maude turned the knob and pushed open the heavy door.

We all stepped into the condo like storm troopers on a mission. One glance around confirmed Parker wasn't home at the moment. The same cheap rental furniture filled the living room. We stood in the middle of the apartment. I looked for printed photographs of my family. Maude had no compunctions marching through the unit and poking her nose into the bedrooms and baths.

"Who really owns this condo?" asked Colleen.

Maude inspected the dirty dishes in the kitchen sink, looked inside the refrigerator then turned to answer Colleen. "A very sweet elderly gentleman, Henry Dobkins. He's staying with his daughter on Nantucket while this place is being renovated or was supposed to be. Clearly this John Parker is a squatter, although I have no idea how he secured a key." She swept her hand around the room. "And this junk ... oh my goodness. Henry would have a heart attack if he saw his lovely residence filled with this trash."

"We definitely need to tell Doug and Sergeant Drake. Obviously, John Parker—if that's even his name—is breaking the law by being here. The question is why is he here and why is he spying on us and taking secret photographs?"

Chapter Eight

Monumental Meeting

F inally!

We kept our promise to the boys to tour the monument. Our trio of golf carts bounced along the trail leading to the island isthmus and the 352 foot-tall Perry's Monument. The Peace Memorial rose majestically with the waves of Lake Erie as its backdrop. Swarms of people mingled at its base, posed for pictures, and listened to the park rangers explain the history and significance of the monument.

We parked the carts then strolled to the base of the tower to hear the thrilling recitation of the sea battle where Commodore Oliver Perry defeated the British invasion of our infant country in 1812. Our boys listened enthralled as the ranger explained how the Battle of Lake Erie sent the British fleet back to England. This was a piece of American history that they would remember. They ran toward the entrance to climb the tower stairs up to the observation deck.

"You go ahead, Harold and I will stay here on this nice shady bench," Maude said with an imperial wave of her hand.

I nodded to her as I joined Anna and Colleen and headed toward the monument entrance.

"C'mon, let's take the elevator to the top. Let Doug and Ron climb those stairs with the boys," I suggested.

"Yep. I'm too old to play mountain goat," Chuck said as he stepped into the elevator.

The elevator whisked us to the top. We waited for several minutes for Doug and Ron to join us on the deck. The boys giggled and ran to the lookout binoculars while the men panted and wheezed, trying to catch their breaths after the long climb.

"Think you better ride the elevator down with us old folks," I said with a chuckle, patting my husband on the back.

The panoramic view from that height was amazing. Canada lay on the horizon and below us, the marina stretched along the shoreline. The boats bobbed like tiny toys in the water. I stood leaning against the tall ledge and gazed down into the park beneath us. A man separated from a crowd of tourists and moved toward an empty bench. He raised his head to stare upwards at the tower and as he did so, I recognized the visage of John Parker. I swear our eyes met and held as he realized I had spotted him.

"Doug ... look down there. That's John Parker. He's here. That's no coincidence. Let's get down. We need to talk to that man."

"Are you sure that's him? From this height, how can you be positive?"

"It's him. Trust me. C'mon," I said. I turned to Anna and Colleen. "We're grabbing the elevator to go down. We've spotted Parker. Will you stay and make sure the boys all get down safely?"

"Of course, sugar. Y'all be careful," Anna drawled.

As soon as the elevator doors opened, Doug and I squeezed past the other tourists and rushed out of the lobby toward where I'd seen Parker. I grabbed Doug's arm and pointed to a man casually walking away from the picnic area. Parker glanced over his shoulder and saw us coming; he picked up his pace.

Harold and Maude watched us as we pursued the suspect.

"That's Parker!" I shouted to Maude, in answer to her puzzled expression as the man approached where they had been waiting.

Just as Parker ran down the sidewalk toward the parking lot, Maude stood up and swung her heavy tote bag at the man's legs. He stumbled and fell to the ground. Doug sprinted forward to capture the man before he could gain his footing and get away.

I laughed at the smug expression on my mother-in-law's face. "Well done, Maude! I couldn't have done better myself."

"Hmph. I expect some answers from that gentleman. What business does he have staying in Henry's apartment?" Maude demanded.

"I'd like some answers too. Like why is he photographing my family? Who is this guy?" I asked.

Doug yanked Parker to his feet and led him away from the crowd of gawkers toward one of the more secluded picnic tables. He shoved him toward the bench seat then stared at the man. Maude and I stood next to him.

"All right, buddy, start talking. Who are you and why are you following me?" Doug asked in a taut voice. He propped one foot on the bench next to Park, effectively trapping him.

Parker squirmed in his seat. He glanced at me and Maude then back at Doug. He finally cracked under our combined pressure.

"I was hired. Okay? Some guy paid me to take photos of your family —said it was for a 'security check.' I didn't ask questions."

"Who was it?" I pressed before Doug could get a word in. My racing pulse had nothing to do with my dash across the lawn moments earlier.

"I don't know his name. The money was good; that's all I cared about. He told me to focus on your husband. That's all I know, I swear!"

Doug spoke into his cell phone, then turned back to the defeated man. "Did you tamper with the brakes on our golf cart at the condo?"

"No! I swear."

"You're doing a lot of swearing. How did you get paid? Who did you call to report my movements?"

Maude broke into the conversation, "I want to know how you got a key to that condo. Who gave it to you?"

Parker's face turned red and he visibly shrunk under Maude's glare. The woman could have intimidated terrorists with that look. Even I felt nervous, watching her give this guy her evil eye.

"Maurice ... Maurice gave me the key. He arranged for the furniture to be moved into the empty apartment and said I could stay there. I paid him. It was just business."

I imagined steam rising from my mother-in-law's head. If looks could kill ... well it would be all over for John Parker and I wouldn't put any money on Maurice's well being either. I tried to remember where I had heard the name Maurice. Of course, the rental agent that met us and gave us the keys. Nope. I wouldn't give you a plug nickel for Maurice's chances of keeping his job or staying out of jail.

Parker clammed up as Put-in-Bay's single police cruiser arrived with Sergeant Drake. The young policeman hurried to our sides and Doug filled him in on the suspect at hand.

Drake and Doug stepped away as Maude and I kept Parker in custody.

"Sounds like the best we can hold him on might be unlawful squatting, maybe voyeurism. You said he got the key from the rental agent, so he didn't break in. It's not illegal to take pictures; he could claim you happened to appear in the background."

"I know. It's pretty slim. But do me a favor and book him at least for the night. I need to know who hired him."

Our group gathered together as we watched Drake load Parker into the cruiser. I think it was safe to say that we all breathed a sigh of relief as we climbed aboard our golf carts. We headed toward the concert location on the other side of the marina. After the excitement at the monument, relaxing during a two hour concert seemed like an excellent idea.

Chapter Nine

Swing, Swing, Swing

The open-air amphitheater buzzed with energy as the crowd settled into their seats, the soft hum of conversation mixing with the rustling of programs and the occasional scrape of a folding chair. A cool breeze drifted in from Lake Erie, carrying the fresh, damp scent of the water, its crisp edge a reminder that evening had arrived. The amphitheater's stone seating rose in a graceful arc, surrounding a wide, well-lit stage. A full orchestra tuned their instruments in anticipation of the night's performance—a tribute to the timeless music of Glenn Miller and Benny Goodman.

"Well, isn't this just grand?" Anna drawled, her Texan twang cutting through the air like a whip crack as she climbed the steps and settled into her seat next to me. She fluffed her light cardigan dramatically and glanced around. "I reckon this is fancier than any hoedown I ever attended back home. And no hay bales in sight."

"Watch your knees, Anna," Chuck said dryly from her other side, leaning back into his seat. "They're not as young as they used to be."

Anna swatted his arm with a playful grin. "Well, aren't you just a peach, Chuck Thompson. If my knees quit on me, I'll just roll right down to the stage and ask that good-looking trombone player to carry me back up."

Chuck raised an eyebrow at his wife; I hid my grin behind my hand. Anna always gave as good as she got.

The sun dipped lazily toward the horizon, splashing streaks of orange and pink across the sky. Laughter and chatter rolled through the air like waves, punctuated by bursts of tuning instruments on stage. The scent of the lake mingled with the aroma of popcorn and sizzling bratwursts from nearby food carts. I breathed in deeply, letting the moment calm my nerves and soothe my worries.

"You know," I said to Doug as we settled onto the concrete risers, "If someone could bottle this scent—brats, kettle corn, and sunscreen—they'd have a bestseller."

Doug grunted, shifting on the hard surface. "I think it already exists. It's called Eau de Tourist Trap."

"Whew, this breeze is a lifesaver. I thought I was gonna melt clean away like a popsicle. Must be having one of those hot flashes," Anna said as she wiped the back of her neck with a napkin.

"Like an ice sculpture at a summer wedding," Colleen added, earning a round of groans and chuckles from everyone.

I observed Maude carefully place a soft cushion on the unforgiving, hard seat in the row ahead of us. Wishing I had brought one myself, I envied her cushy tushy. Guess Maude deserved the comfortable seat after single-handedly tackling our suspect. The memory of her swinging that heavy tote made me laugh out loud, causing several heads to turn my way.

Anna snorted and let out a bark of laughter as she read my mind. She leaned forward and tapped Maude on the shoulder.

"I tell you what, Maude, you've got spunk. I'd pay good money to see that swing you made this afternoon on replay."

"Just call it a reflex," Maude said innocently, though I caught the wink she threw my way.

Colleen chimed in, "You'll be getting offers to join the local softball team."

Doug's voice broke through our merriment, low and serious. "Let's not forget what Parker was really up to. Someone hired him to keep an eye on us—on me, specifically. If we don't figure this out soon, it's only going to get worse."

The weight of his words settled over us like a shadow. I caught Maude's gaze and saw the unspoken worry in her eyes. Despite her earlier heroics, she knew as well as I did how dangerous this situation was getting for her son.

"What did you get out of Parker when you questioned him?" Harold asked, his voice calm but sharp.

Doug sighed and ran a hand through his hair. "Not much. I didn't speak with him very long. It's up to Drake to interrogate him. Parker's just the errand boy—someone paid him to spy on us and take photos. He doesn't know who's behind the real threat or so he says."

"Are you still looking for that bartender?" asked Ron.

"Yeah. Drake is bringing over the photos from the video he downloaded off the winery cameras. I'm hoping we can show the pictures around town and find someone who recognizes the guy."

Chuck shook his head slowly. "Someone really wants you out of the picture, Doug. This isn't amateur stuff."

Doug's jaw tightened. "No, it's not. And that's what worries me."

A hush fell over our group.

"So what do we do?" Maude asked softly, her voice surprisingly steady.

Doug looked at her, then at all of us. "We stay alert. And we stick together. I don't want anyone wandering off alone."

"Ain't nobody splitting up, I can promise you that," Anna drawled. She gave me a pointed look. "That goes double for you, Merry. I'm stickin' to you like a burr on a dog's tail."

I couldn't help but laugh. "You're saying I'm the dog in this scenario?"

"I said what I said," she replied with a grin.

The boys—Johnny, Billy, and Stevie—giggled as they huddled together, peering at the orchestra pit and whispering about the enormous tuba they could see gleaming under the stage lights.

The crowd's murmurs softened as the conductor stepped onto the podium, and a hush fell over the amphitheater. With a crisp wave of his baton, the orchestra launched into a lively rendition of Glenn Miller's "In the Mood." The rich, brassy notes of the big band sound swept over the audience, filling the cool air with its infectious rhythm.

"Now this is music," Harold said, tapping his foot to the beat. "Not that racket you hear on the radio nowadays."

The music shifted, now a smooth, nostalgic rendition of Benny Goodman's "Sing, Sing, Sing," the pounding rhythm of the drums filling the amphitheater. Couples were already swaying in their seats, some even standing to dance in the aisles.

"Oh, Harold!" Maude exclaimed, tugging her husband's hand. "Let's dance!"

Harold groaned but stood dutifully, allowing Maude to drag him toward a small open space by the aisle where other couples had gathered.

Anna laughed, clapping her hands. "Well, look at them go! Chuck, you and I need to follow suit before we get out-danced by a sexagenarian."

Chuck stood with a long-suffering sigh. "Come on, woman. Let's show them how it's done."

I watched as my friends and in-laws twirled to the music. Anna's laughter rang out like a bell. The boys had abandoned their seats to stand at the edge of the stone rows, watching the dancers and egging on their grandparents with hoots and cheers.

Doug sat back, though his hand remained firmly on my knee. "You think we'll be dancing like that when we're their age?"

"Of course," I said with a grin. "But I'll lead."

Doug shook his head with a small smile, but said nothing. His eyes flickered back to the crowd. I noticed it immediately.

"Doug?"

"Parker," he said under his breath. "Third row up. By the aisle."

I turned my head casually, as though admiring the amphitheater's stone archways. Sure enough, there he was—John Parker, wearing an ill-fitting hat pulled low over his face, watching us with all the subtlety of a hawk eyeing prey.

"Why didn't Drake hold him? He's got some nerve showing up here."

"I've got to admit, Parker's boldness bothers me. I didn't think he'd still be under payroll to continue spying on us. What's his game?" Doug commented as he stared at the man, all interest in the lively music fading away.

The orchestra swelled into its final, triumphant notes, the crowd erupted in applause. Chuck whistled a high shrill sound in appreciation. For us, our interest stayed on the figure three rows up.

Doug reached over and gave my hand a squeeze, his thumb tracing over my knuckles.

"We'll get to the bottom of this, Merry," he murmured.

"I know we will," I said, my voice soft but firm. "They have no idea who they're messing with."

Chapter Ten

Hurricane Maude

"Four days on this island and I haven't caught a fish yet. C'mon guys, let's get our poles in the water and catch tonight's supper," declared Chuck as he placed his coffee cup on the counter.

Colleen had knocked on our door earlier that morning to invite all of us to their condo for breakfast. Anna had cooked an impromptu breakfast buffet. We gathered around the dining table and countertop buffet, filling our plates with fluffy pancakes, delicious scrambled eggs, crisp bacon and mouth-watering sausage patties, along with a large bowl of fruit salad.

"Everything is wonderful," Maude said as she sampled another serving of eggs. "If you and Merry provide food of this caliber to your guests, I can understand why your tea shop has been so successful."

"Thank you. That's very kind of you to say," replied Anna.

"I didn't know you were aware of our shop," I said.

"I keep tabs on my family. You've become quite the entrepreneur, Meredith. Harold and I are both proud of you."

My mouth fell open and you could have knocked me over with a feather. My face must have reflected my thoughts because Anna rushed to slide a chair under me. I was speechless.

"What do you say we take the kids down to the beach? The guys can get in some fishing while we ladies enjoy some sand and sun," asked Colleen as she stepped in to change the conversation.

With mouths full of food, the guys all mumbled their approval from the corner of the kitchen where they had congregated to speak in low voices of manly things.

"Perfect. Harold and I will show you the best beach that affords some privacy and the men can fish in the surf."

"You're coming?" I asked.

"Of course. I like a day at the beach. I'll put up an umbrella though to keep from getting sun burned," Maude said. "But first, Merry, we have something we need to do."

"We do?"

I raised an eyebrow at this bit of news until I read the determined look on her face and nodded my agreement. Her statement was a command I couldn't ignore. Besides, if she was planning what I thought she was, I definitely wanted to be there.

"Great! We'll all put on swimsuits and pack our gear," Anna said. "Colleen and I'll get this stuff cleaned up in a jiffy."

"Billy and Johnny, when you finish your plates, go over and get dressed for the beach. Make sure you wear t-shirts and grab that tube of sun screen or you'll both look like red lobsters by the end of the day."

Doug's phone rang as I snapped the lid on the container of fruit salad. Our eyes met in silent communication.

"Be right back. I'm running down to the police station to pick up those photographs from Drake."

"All right. Be careful. We'll be ready to leave when you get back," I said. "Right now your mother and I have an errand to run."

"You and my mother? Wonders never cease. I won't even ask what you're up to," Doug said with a chuckle.

"Hmm, better that you don't, I think."

Maude marched toward the door. She smiled at the boys, then with a nod to me, headed into the hall. I tossed the dish towel onto the counter and hurried after her. She had already pressed the elevator button and stood tapping her foot impatiently. I had to dash to step into the waiting elevator before the door slid closed.

The morning sun poured into the glass-walled lobby of the high-rise condominium, glinting off polished marble floors and lending the air a deceptive serenity. I stood just behind Maude, who was clearly in her element, radiating a commanding presence that would've cowed most people. Her pearl necklace glimmered as she leaned on the counter, fixing the rental agent, Maurice Dillard, with a look sharp enough to slice through the tension in the room.

Maurice, a slight man in his mid-fifties with a thin mustache and a balding crown, fidgeted behind the desk. His shirt collar was too tight, his tie crooked, and beads of sweat collected at his temples. The pen he held trembled slightly, tapping a nervous staccato against the polished granite surface.

Maude wasn't one to waste time. "Mr. Dillard," she began, her voice crisp and deliberate, "would you care to explain why a certain Mr. John Parker was found living in Henry Dobkins' condo? A condo he had no business accessing, I might add."

Maurice swallowed hard, his Adam's apple bobbing visibly. "Mrs. Gardner, I—I assure you, I wouldn't knowingly—"

"You knowingly handed over a key to an unauthorized person," Maude interrupted, her tone unwavering. "That's negligence at best, conspiracy at worst. Which is it?"

I stepped closer, folding my arms but letting Maude take the lead. She was like a well-dressed hurricane: composed on the surface, devastating underneath.

Maurice shifted uncomfortably. "I didn't think it would be a problem. Mr. Parker said he was ... an old friend of the family. He ... he just needed a place to stay for a week or two."

"An old friend?" Maude repeated, arching an eyebrow. "And you didn't think to verify this with the actual residents or me as HOA secretary?"

"Well, he seemed very convincing, and he—" Maurice stammered, tugging at his tie.

"Maurice," I interjected gently, my voice softer but still firm, "you do realize that your actions put my husband and my children at risk? Not to mention everyone else in this building. John Parker isn't anyone's friend; he's been spying on us. And worse. He may be an accessory to murder."

Maurice gulped at the word murder; his face flushed a deep red. He looked down at the counter as if it might somehow rescue him. "I-I didn't know! He—he paid me to let him in. A little something extra on the side, you know? I needed—"

"Save it." Maude cut him off with a wave of her hand. "You've admitted to gross misconduct. I'll be filing a formal complaint with the home owner's association, demanding your immediate dismissal."

Maurice's mouth opened and closed like a fish gasping for air. "But Mrs. Gardner, please! I've been here fifteen years!"

"Then you should have known better," Maude snapped. "Fifteen years, and you've just destroyed whatever trust you'd built. How many other 'little extras' have you taken over the years, Maurice?"

I watched Maurice's shoulders slump, his hands clenching the edge of the desk. "I swear, this was the only time! I made a mistake—"

"Mistakes have consequences," Maude said icily. She straightened her pearl necklace with an air of finality and turned to me. "Merry, would you be so kind as to call the local police? I believe they should be present to witness Mr. Parker's eviction from the premises. And Mr. Dillard's. I'll need to quickly find a replacement for him."

Maurice looked like he might melt into the floor. "Police? Isn't that a little extreme? I mean, I can't lose my job over this! I need—"

"What you need," Maude interrupted with a saccharine smile, "is a reminder that people's safety is more important than a few extra dollars. Consider this your lesson. You will also make arrangements to remove that hideous furniture and debris from Henry's unit."

I stepped back and pulled out my phone, dialing the station. "Hi, this is Merry Gardner," I said when the officer picked up. "We need an officer at the Lakeview Condos. There's a situation involving unauthorized access to a unit."

Maurice looked like he might cry, but Maude remained impervious. "Now," she said, lowering her voice but losing none of its steel, "I suggest you sit quietly and wait for the authorities. Any attempt to leave will only make this worse."

As I hung up the phone, I couldn't help but admire her. "You really don't pull punches, do you?" I murmured.

Maude gave a small, satisfied smile. "When it comes to my family's safety or my responsibilities, absolutely not. From what I hear, you do the same."

"Remind me never to get on your bad side," I quipped, earning a rare chuckle from her.

The police arrived not long after, their presence lending an air of gravity to the situation. Maurice shrank further under their scrutiny, and I almost felt sorry for him—almost. Maude calmly explained the situation, her voice steady and authoritative. Drake's two officers nodded, taking notes and assuring us they'd handle John Parker's removal.

As the officers escorted Maurice away for questioning, I turned to Maude. "You were amazing back there," I said. "I think even Doug would've been impressed."

She patted my arm, her usual sternness softening. "Well, dear, when you've raised three children and dealt with Harold's antics for fifty years, you learn how to manage a little crisis now and then."

I laughed, shaking my head. "I think you missed your calling as a police chief."

She gave me a sly smile. "And take all the fun away from Douglas? Never."

The police cruiser had just pulled away as Doug wheeled the golf cart into the carport. He glanced at the departing car then focused his attention on us as he hurried toward the condo office.

"What's going on? Is everyone all right?"

"Everything is under control, son. Maurice just explained how John Parker gained access to Henry's apartment and now Mr. Parker has been officially evicted and Maurice has been dismissed from his position."

"Your mother called a locksmith and the locks are being changed on that condo unit too. John Parker won't be residing there if he dares to come back. You should have seen Maude in action," I explained with an admiring glance at his mother.

"Sounds like you two have been busy. Now I understand why you said I wouldn't want to know about your little errand."

"Did you get the photos from Drake?" I asked.

"Yeah, I got them. They're a bit grainy, printed off the winery security camera, but you can make out the guy's features."

Doug handed me a brown envelope and I dug out the photographs. As I scanned the first two shots, I paused, studying the closeup of an older, tall man with dark hair and a thin mustache. Dressed in a white shirt and black vest with a string bow tie similar to the other wait staff at the winery, his face seemed familiar to me. I held the picture up to the light for a better look. Yes, I was sure of it. This was the seaman on board the ferry boat.

"I recognize this man," I said in a hushed voice. My mind spun with a thousand questions. Why would an ordinary seaman pose as a bartender to poison my husband?

Chapter Eleven

Beachy Keen

The secluded beach curved like a crescent moon, framed by towering swamp white oak trees. Pungent bay laurel swayed in the gentle breeze, shading the rocky path that led down to the sandy beach. The scent of damp earth and sun-warmed wood mingled with the smells of sand, water, and sunscreen. Lake Erie waves lapped rhythmically against the shore. It was a slice of paradise—if only we weren't constantly reminded that danger loomed over our heads like a dark cloud.

We spread out blankets and arranged lawn chairs on the hot sand while Harold positioned the wide umbrella to shade Maude. Sunshine sparkled on the water like glistening diamonds against the dark lake.

Tossing t-shirts onto the blanket, all three boys raced across the blistering sand to the water's edge. I heard a collective sigh of relief as the water cooled their burning feet.

"How deep is the water here? Is it safe for the boys to swim?" I asked.

"They'll be fine as long as they stay close to the beach. There's a sandbar that stretches from the coastline outward about two hundred feet, beyond that the bottom drops off and the lake deepens with a strong current. We'll keep an eye on them and I'll warn them to stay close," Harold answered me. He picked up his fishing gear and joined the other men.

The boys ventured a little further out, their shouts and laughter carried over the gentle breeze. Doug, Harold, Chuck, and Ron stood ankle-deep in the lake, casting their lines and discussing the finer points of bait and tackle. I glanced over to where Maude and my friends lounged in beach chairs, slathering on sunscreen and stretching legs in the sun's rays. Each of us pretended to be more relaxed than we really were.

Anna, her cowgirl hat tilted low over her eyes, sighed. "Well, ladies, nothing says vacation like murder plots and mysterious photographs. Am I right, or am I right?" She laughed, bringing up the subject we were all trying to avoid. She looked pointedly at me.

"Spot on," I replied dryly, leaning back and letting the sun warm my skin. "I just love being a target for assassins. Really makes the whole getaway vibe complete."

Colleen twittered nervously. Her smile faded as she peered at the grainy photos we'd been poring over. She passed the photo back to my mother-in-law. "So, Maude, you're sure that's him?"

Maude, ever the picture of poise, nodded solemnly. "That's Walter Kowalski. No doubt about it. Of course he's older than the last time I saw him, but that's him. You don't forget someone who ruined your husband's business and destroyed your source of income. Harold and I both got jobs elsewhere to make ends meet. We depleted our savings account making mortgage and car payments to maintain our credit history. It took us five years to get back on our feet."

The name hung in the air, heavy with implications. Walter Kowalski. A man Harold and Maude hadn't spoken of in decades. I turned to her, curious. "What's the complete story?"

She sighed, smoothing the hem of her silk halter top and brushing grains of sand off white linen shorts. "Walter was Harold's business partner back when we first married. They owned an electronics company together. Everything was fine until Harold discovered Walter had been stealing inventory and embezzling money—substantial sums. By the time it all came to light, the company was on the brink of bankruptcy. Harold filed charges. Walter was arrested, convicted, and sent to prison."

"For how long?" Anna asked, squinting at the photo as if staring at it hard enough would reveal answers.

"Ten years," Maude replied. "We heard he got out after serving his term, but we lost track of him. That was close to twenty years ago."

Harold wandered up from the lakeshore, his fishing rod in hand, and joined our conversation. At my questioning glance toward his rod, he shrugged. "Fish aren't biting. Walter disappeared after prison. He never tried to contact us, and we were happy to leave it that way."

"Until now," I murmured, looking back at the photo. Walter's features were blurred but distinct enough—piercing eyes above a sharp nose on an older man with dark hair and a thin mustache.

"I'm pretty sure I saw him on the ferry when we arrived. He wore coveralls and worked on the deck," I explained.

Doug, who had followed Harold up the beach, wiped his hands on a towel and frowned. "Why didn't you mention it then?"

"Because I didn't think anything of it at the time," I admitted, feeling a small twinge of guilt. "It's a ferry. People work on boats. You saw him when we stood near the bow. The man coiled ropes and readied the gangway. He didn't seem out of place or unusual to warrant my attention. I just wish I had paid more attention to the bartender at the winery and recognized him then."

Harold exchanged a worried glance with Maude. "If it really is Walter, he's had decades to hold a grudge. And if he's working with this Parker fellow ..."

"Then he's dangerous," Doug finished grimly.

Anna shook her head. "So let me get this straight. This guy Kowalski embezzled from Harold, went to prison, and now, years later, he's mixed up in a plot to poison Doug and take out the whole Gardner family?"

"Looks like it," I said. "The question is, why? Revenge? Money? Both? And why now and here?"

Colleen tapped her chin thoughtfully. "And how is John Parker connected? Did Kowalski hire him? Are they partners?"

"Good questions," Doug said, his brow furrowed. "And ones we need answers to."

"All this time, I thought someone from Doug's law enforcement past was stirring up trouble. I never imagined the threat went deeper into the family's past," I said. My brow wrinkled into a worried frown.

The sound of the boys' laughter rang out again, momentarily lightening the mood. Billy, Johnny, and Stevie were splashing each other, carefree and oblivious to the undercurrent of tension among the adults. I watched them frolic. Ah ... to be young like that again. A smile curved my lips. For their sake, I tried to push the darker thoughts aside, but it wasn't easy.

"What's our next move?" Maude asked, ever practical.

Doug crossed his arms, his stance firm. "Now that we know who we're looking for, I'll start digging into Walter's whereabouts and connections. Make some calls back home, see if my deputy, Tony, can learn what Kowalski's been up to since his release. He can run a background check, confirm his employment and residency."

"Aren't you going to inform the local police, Sergeant Drake, that you identified the suspect?" asked Ron.

"I will, as soon as I learn more about him. I don't know Ron. Something feels off. My gut tells me to keep it close to the vest for the time being."

"And in the meantime?" Anna pressed.

"We stay vigilant, like I said before," Doug replied, his tone leaving no room for argument.

Maude placed a hand on her hip, her lips pursed. "Vigilant, yes. But

I think we need to be proactive too. If Walter is on this island, he won't stay hidden forever."

Harold nodded in agreement. "Maude's right. If there's one thing I know about Walter, it's that he's not the type to back down once he's set his sights on something."

I stared out at the lake. The water shimmered under the midday sun. It was beautiful, tranquil—everything this vacation was supposed to be. But the peace was fragile, threatened by shadows from the family's past.

"I just hope we can figure this out before anyone else gets hurt," I said softly.

Maude reached over and gave my hand a reassuring squeeze. "We will, Merry. Gardners persevere and protect our own."

Her confidence was comforting, but the unease lingered. Somewhere out there, Walter Kowalski was watching, waiting, and plotting.

We may have thwarted him by spoiling John Parker's spy operation, but until we fully stopped him, none of us could truly relax. I knew one thing for sure: this killer would not get away with it. Not on our watch. Our resolve grew as we stared at the photo in my hand.

Chapter Twelve

Amelia

Early the next morning, a light knock on our condo door drew my attention. I paused, the brewed coffee pot in my hand, then placed the pot back on its burner. Stepping to the door, I cautiously cracked it open. A pleasant-looking middle-aged woman, her soft brown hair gathered into a ponytail, waited with a younger girl. Both wore gray uniforms with white aprons. I opened the door wider and greeted the two women.

"Hello. I'm Amelia. May I speak with Mrs. Gardner?"

"Of course. Please come in."

Hearing voices in the living room, Maude walked out of her bedroom and joined me. She smiled and nodded in greeting to Amelia.

"Meredith, this is Amelia Green. She's housekeeper for the complex and oversees the cleaning staff. Amelia, this is my daughter-in-law. My family is visiting this week," Maude said by way of introductions.

"I recalled Maurice mentioning there were occupants in your suite and next door in number four. That's why I stopped by. Do you need me to clean the full apartment as usual or would you prefer just a quick bathroom and kitchen refresh?" She motioned to the girl next to her.

"Betty's here and can perform a quick maid service if it won't intrude on your day."

"Yes, I'd appreciate that. Harold took my son and grandsons out for a day of fishing, so it's just Merry and me at home. By all means, Betty, you can start in the master bath. The room's empty." Maude gestured to Amelia to take a seat at the breakfast bar. "Coffee? Merry and I were just about to have a cup. I'm glad you've stopped by. I wanted to speak with you."

I caught Amelia glance questioningly at me, then Maude as she slid onto a bar stool. "Coffee would be nice. Black. Thank you," she said in a soft voice.

Maude poured herself a mug then served a hot cup to the house-keeper. I picked up my cup, freshened it with a splash of hot coffee, then grabbed a yogurt from the refrigerator before joining them. Amelia appeared nervous, her white knuckles tightly gripping the mug handle. Maude's next words surprised her and me.

"How would you like to serve as the rental agent for the complex? I'm sure you're aware that I fired Maurice. I won't go into details of why. The HOA is cognizant of your professional supervisory skills of the staff: both cleaning and maintenance crews. You've been doing far more than your position calls for without being asked. It's about time the condo management compensated you for your work. Don't you agree?"

Amelia grinned broadly. She clasped Maude's hand and shook it vigorously. Her actions startled the unflappable Maude, who suddenly appeared flustered. I hid a chuckle behind my raised coffee mug. Even I wasn't comfortable grabbing my mother-in-law's hand so freely.

"Do you think you can manage the staff while taking on the duties of rental agent? I need someone dependable to oversee the condo complex, especially when the residents are gone. Want the job?" asked Maude.

"Yes, máam. When would you like me to start?" Amelia beamed her pleasure.

"Suppose we go down to the office later this morning and you can become familiar with the record keeping and I can sort through the receipts Maurice left behind."

"That would be perfect, Mrs. Gardner. I'll have time to oversee the cleaning necessary on this floor and direct my staff on the other floors too. Thank you for this opportunity. I won't let you down."

"I know you won't. And Amelia ... thank you for taking the job. We're lucky to have you."

Amelia finished her coffee then rushed down the hall to speak with Betty. She left our unit, and I heard her knock on Anna's door to introduce herself and offer her cleaning service.

I studied my mother-in-law then on impulse, wrapped my arms around her in a brief hug.

"Goodness! All this emotion, and so early in the morning too." She raised an eyebrow at me but didn't pull away.

I think she rather liked my display of affection.

"That was really nice of you. Bet she does a better job than Maurice."

"I'm sure she will. But I meant it. Amelia should have been paid a higher salary long ago. She's earned it."

Maude and I rapped on the door. Colleen and Anna scooped up handbags and rushed to join us in the hall as we all headed to the waiting elevator.

"This will be so much fun," Colleen said as we glided toward the lobby.

"I'm looking forward to some girl time. How about you?" I asked my friends.

"Absolutely! Let's get this party on the roll," drawled Anna.

"I found the perfect shops in town off the main street that you gals will love. I'm sure you'll find some treasures," Maude said as we exited the building and headed for the carport.

Skies were blue and cloudless while the sun shone brightly. I took that as a good sign. Laughter filled the air as we piled into Maude's candy-apple-red golf cart for a jaunt into town. A quick flash of hurtling toward the cliff sprang to my mind as I settled into the front seat with Maude behind the wheel. The mechanic, Charlie, had assured both Harold and Doug that the cart was safe to drive, but I couldn't help taking a deep breath as we prepared to leave.

"Hold on, ladies," Maude said with a chuckle, adjusting her over-sized sunhat with one hand and gripping the wheel with the other. "This might get bumpy."

I stared at my mother-in-law. I'd never seen her so playful before. It was like being with an entirely new person ... one that I liked very much. Whether it was the sunny carefree day or sitting behind the wheel of that silly golf cart, but Maude seemed twenty years younger and giddy.

I exchanged a glance with Colleen, who muttered, "I should've brought a helmet."

The cart lurched forward with a jerk, and we bounced down the gravel path from the condos, the breeze whipping through our hair. Fragrant bay laurel trees lined the narrow roads, beyond them gave way to glimpses of Lake Erie's shimmering blue waters. The air smelled of fresh spice and damp earth, mingling with the faint sweetness of island wildflowers growing alongside the road.

Anna, perched precariously in the backseat with Colleen, held onto the side rail as though her life depended on it. "If we survive this ride, I'll buy everyone ice cream," she declared in her thick Texan drawl.

"You're on," Colleen replied, laughing.

We reached the main strip of town, a charming collection of historic storefronts with weathered shingles and colorful awnings. The shops were a mix of craft boutiques, antique stores, and local eateries, each more inviting than the last. Maude turned up a narrow side street then parked the golf cart with a flourish—or rather, screeched to a halt that left us all clutching the seats.

"I do love a woman who knows how to make an entrance," Anna quipped, hopping out and adjusting her wide-brimmed cowgirl hat. "Mmm, this place smells like an Italian restaurant. I feel like there ought to be a pot of spaghetti sauce simmering somewhere."

"That's the bay laurel trees that line the street. You can pick the leaves and take some home, fresh bay leaves just like the packaged spices in the market," explained Maude.

We started with the craft shops, wandering through aisles of hand-made soaps, pottery, and whimsical garden décor. Colleen found a set of painted coasters featuring local landmarks, while Maude haggled over a hand-carved walking stick she didn't need but "couldn't live without."

"Are you buying that walking stick for Harold or do you need a solid bat for your next encounter?" I joked.

"Hmm, I hadn't thought of that, but I suppose both." Maude gave me a wink and proceeded to take her solid oak stick to the cashier.

In the antique store, Anna unearthed a peculiar collection of porcelain cow figurines, holding one up with a smirk. "Think Chuck would like this for the mantle?"

"He might, but don't be surprised if you see it mysteriously disappear one day," I said, grinning.

"Y'all think so? They're kind of cute, reminds me of Texan cows on the range," Anna said as she fingered the figures.

I browsed through a shelf of delicate tea cups and teapots. A cream-colored porcelain teapot painted with pale blue hydrangea blooms caught my eye. I picked it up and examined the details and knew I had to have it.

"Oh Anna, look at this! Won't it be just perfect for our shop? I love the colors and pattern on this pot."

"Do you see any matching cups and saucers?" asked Anna. "Maybe we could sell it as a set."

"It's too pretty to sell. I want to display it near that wreath you decorated with hydrangeas. It would be nice to find some matching cups and saucers though. Let's keep looking."

By the time we finished shopping, the late afternoon sun was high, and we were ready for a break. We stumbled into a pastel-painted ice cream parlor called The Sweet Spot. It was impossibly cute, with gingham tablecloths, cheerful yellow walls, and an old-fashioned soda fountain. The sugary scent of waffle cones and chocolate permeated the air.

"Jeez Louise! I can feel the calories plastering onto my hips just standing here inhaling all this sweetness," I said.

We each ordered indulgent treats—Colleen got a towering hot fudge sundae, Maude chose a cherry milkshake, Anna opted for a banana split, and I couldn't resist a cone of double chocolate chip swirl. We settled into a corner booth, the cool air conditioning a welcome relief from the heat outside.

As we dug into our desserts, Maude set her spoon down and leaned forward, her expression thoughtful.

"We need to talk about Walter Kowalski and John Parker. I found a note in the office that Maurice made on the date Parker moved in plus a receipt for furniture rental. The timing doesn't sit right with me."

Colleen raised an eyebrow. "You mean how Parker was at the condo a week before we arrived? What was he doing there that long?"

Anna nodded, a dollop of whipped cream on her spoon. "Exactly. And how'd they connect in the first place? It's not like Kowalski put an ad in the classifieds looking for a spy."

I licked a drip from my cone and frowned. "Parker had to have known who we were before we got here. He wasn't just scouting random families on vacation."

"Do you think Walter sent him?" Colleen asked.

"Probably," Maude said, her voice firm. "But what puzzles me is how Parker would've known so much about our plans. Maurice said he didn't share our booking details with anyone, but I'm starting to doubt his honesty."

I snorted. "Maurice couldn't lie convincingly if his life depended on it. You saw how sweaty he got when you confronted him, Maude. The man looked ready to faint."

Maude chuckled. "He did look a bit green around the gills, didn't he? But if Maurice was involved, I doubt he was masterminding anything. More likely, Kowalski dangled some money under his nose and told him to look the other way."

Anna leaned forward, resting her elbows on the table. "If Parker was spying on us for Walter, it means this wasn't a spur-of-the-moment thing. Walter's been planning something for a while."

"And Parker was his eyes and ears," Colleen added, dipping her spoon into the remains of the hot fudge sauce.

"Let's not get ahead of ourselves. Think about it. First of all, this entire trip was a spur of the moment decision. Two weeks ago, I had no idea Doug and I would drive up to Lake Erie. And you all certainly had no plans to be here until the very last minute. How could Kowalski possibly plan in advance if we didn't even know ourselves that we'd be here?" I put the question to my friends.

"That's true. Even Maurice didn't know I had invited my family here until the day before your arrival when I called him with instructions about the keys," Maude said. She stared out the window.

Anna tapped her spoon against her bowl, her tone serious despite the whipped cream mustache she was sporting. "The big question is: Why? What's Walter's endgame? He's been out of prison for years. Why come after Harold and the family now?"

"Maybe because he could. We suddenly turn up right under his nose. How could he resist?" I speculated.

Maude's eyes darkened. "Because he's bitter and desperate. He lost everything he cared about, and in his twisted mind, Harold's to blame. I think he's convinced himself that taking away Harold's family will even the score."

The table fell silent for a moment, the weight of Maude's words settling over us.

"Still doesn't explain Parker," I said finally. "What's his connection to Walter? Was he just a hired hand, or is there more to it? Does anyone think it's hinky that Sgt. Drake didn't hold Parker in jail? What's Parker up to now?"

Colleen tapped her chin thoughtfully. "Parker doesn't strike me as the loyal type. If Kowalski brought him in, it was probably for money. But who's to say Parker didn't have his own agenda?"

Anna grinned. "Maybe he thought spying on us would lead to his big break as a private investigator. 'Parker's Private Eyes'—sounds catchy, doesn't it?"

We all laughed, the tension breaking for a moment.

Maude pointed her spoon at Anna, her tone playful but with an edge of determination. "Laugh all you want, but don't underestimate Parker. He knew too much about our movements for it to be coincidence. We need to figure out how he got his information to pass along to Walter."

"And what his next move is," I added, my stomach twisting despite the delicious ice cream.

Anna raised her bowl in a mock toast. "To uncovering the truth, ladies. And to keeping our menfolk out of trouble while we do it."

Maude smirked. "I think that's the hardest part of all."

"You know, I think we should try to track down John Parker and question him ourselves," I said with a determined look.

After finishing our treats, we picked up our packages and headed back to the golf cart. The sun dipped lower in the sky, casting long shadows over the quaint streets. Despite the laughter and camaraderie, an unspoken tension lingered. We didn't have all the answers yet, but one thing was certain: Walter Kowalski and John Parker weren't finished with us.

And we weren't finished with them either.

Chapter Thirteen

Shadows of the Past

Walter Kowalski stood at the edge of the ferry's deck, his hands gripped the rail as the wind tugged at his faded jacket. The rhythmic hum of the engine vibrated beneath his feet, a sound he learned to associate with monotony. The ferry cut smoothly across the gray-blue waters of Lake Erie, carrying tourists and locals to South Bass Island. For most of the passengers, it was a brief escape into a picturesque world of quaint shops and lakefront views. For Walter, it was his penance and his freedom ... free of the stone prison walls that had confined him. Free to feel the wind and spray on his face. Free to be his own man. Penance as he was forced to endure the monotony.

He watched the sun's reflection ripple on the waves, a bitter smile tugging at his lips. Once, he had dreamed of a life like the one these passengers enjoyed. He and Harold Gardner had almost achieved that life together. But dreams were fragile things, easily shattered under the weight of bad choices.

Walter and Harold had been inseparable as young men, bonded by ambition and the promise of a brighter future. They had pooled their meager savings to open an electronics repair business in a small store-front on the outskirts of Cleveland. This was in the late eighties, when the world was on the brink of a technological revolution. Televisions, radios, and the emerging home computer market promised endless opportunities, and for fifteen years, Kowalski & Gardner Electronics thrived.

Harold was the face of the business, personable and trustworthy, with a knack for putting customers at ease. Walter, the quieter of the two, was the technical genius. He could fix anything with wires and circuits, often improvising clever solutions that Harold would boast about to their clients. Together, they were a perfect team—until Walter's demons caught up with him.

Walter had always loved the thrill of gambling. It started innocently enough—a few friendly poker games, a weekend at the racetrack—but the stakes grew higher with each win, and even higher with each loss. The more he lost, the more he drank ... seeking an answer in booze. By the time he realized he was in over his head, he owed more money than he could ever hope to repay. The men he owed weren't the forgiving type. When their threats escalated to broken windows at the shop and a midnight visit to his home, Walter saw only one way out: the business.

He had siphoned funds from their accounts, just enough at first to keep the debt collectors at bay. But gambling debts were a bottomless pit, and soon, the books didn't add up. He stole equipment and sold it on black markets to line his pockets and keep the loan sharks away. Harold confronted him one night in the shop, his voice shaking with disbelief and anger.

"How could you do this to us, Walt? To me?"

Walter couldn't meet his friend's eyes. "I didn't have a choice, Harold. They would've killed me."

"So you decided to kill our business instead? You've ruined us! We're bankrupt."

Harold had given him an ultimatum: turn himself in or he'd report him to the police. Walter chose neither. Instead, he fled, but Harold followed through on his threat. Within weeks, law enforcement arrested, convicted, and sentenced Walter to ten years in prison for embezzlement. Kowalski & Gardner Electronics dissolved shortly after, leaving Harold to rebuild his life from scratch.

Prison was both a punishment and a crucible. Walter's wife, Linda, visited him at first, bringing their daughter Jane and infant son, Aaron. But as the months dragged on, the visits grew less frequent until they stopped altogether. Walter's letters went unanswered, and when he was finally released, he learned from a mutual acquaintance that Linda had filed for divorce and moved out of state with the children. She had taken her maiden name and cut all ties, leaving Walter with nothing but a stack of unopened letters and a festering rage.

For years, Walter drifted, working odd jobs and drowning his sorrows in cheap whiskey. He blamed Harold for everything—the failed business, the prison sentence, the loss of his family. It didn't matter that he had been the architect of his own downfall. In Walter's mind, Harold had betrayed him, and that betrayal became the focus of his bitterness.

When Walter finally found steady work as a deckhand on the ferry, he'd won a small victory. The job was grueling and low-paying, but it gave him a sense of purpose. Being out on the water with the wind in his face gave him a sense of freedom, with no walls to imprison him. The tedious daily round-trips between Port Clinton and Put-in-Bay put money in his pocket, but more importantly, it gave him a connection to a family he thought he had lost for good. The ferry brought him closer to Aaron, who Walter learned resided on the island. Walter never approached his son directly; he wasn't ready for the rejection he knew would come. But he watched from afar, collecting bits of information and treasuring the rare glimpses of the young man who barely knew he existed.

Walter might have continued this quiet, pitiful existence if not for a chance encounter on the ferry. He overheard a conversation between two passengers—a sheriff named Douglas Gardner and his wife discussing their upcoming vacation with his parents on South Bass Island. The name hit him like a thunderclap. Gardner ... Harold Gardner. The man who had destroyed his life.

The discovery reignited Walter's old anger, but this time, it came with an opportunity. If Harold and his family were vacationing on the island, Walter could strike. He didn't know how or when, but he would make them pay for what he had lost.

As the ferry docked at South Bass Island, Walter watched the passengers disembark, his eyes scanning the crowd for any sign of the Gardners. He spotted them easily—a tight-knit group with easy smiles and animated conversation. They looked happy, content, oblivious to the storm brewing just out of sight.

Walter's hands tightened on the rail, his knuckles white. This was his chance. Years of anger, regret, and bitterness had brought him to this moment. And he wasn't about to let it slip away.

He contacted Aaron—his first direct contact in years—and laid out his plan. It wasn't easy to convince him.

Aaron had grown up without his father, raised to despise the man who had failed them. But Walter was persuasive. He painted a picture of Harold as a cold, calculating man who had ruined Walter's life out of spite. He appealed to Aaron's sense of loyalty, reminding him that they were blood. Walter needed an ally on the island, someone who could gather information and help him stay one step ahead of the Gardners.

His son hesitated but eventually agreed, more out of curiosity than conviction. The idea of meeting Harold Gardner, the man in his father's past, intrigued Aaron. If helping Walter gave him that chance, so be it.

He didn't know the full extent of Walter's plan, and Walter didn't share it. For now, it was enough that they were working together.

Walter's plan began with John Parker, a grifter he had met through an old gambling contact. Parker was rough around the edges but reliable when it came to dirty work. Walter had spotted him on the island weeks ago when he had come ashore. Parker had a knack for conning any mark and finagle a cushy place to live before skipping out. He enlisted him to keep tabs on the Gardner family, to observe their movements and report back. He gave Parker explicit instructions to remain inconspicuous, but Parker's arrogance and sloppiness soon drew attention.

Walter's ultimate goal was simple: take from Harold what Harold had taken from him. It didn't matter that Harold had gone on to build a successful life, that he had a family who loved him and a reputation for integrity. Walter wanted to see him suffer, to feel the sting of betrayal and loss that had defined Walter's own existence for so long.

But even as he plotted his revenge, a small part of him wavered. He saw Aaron in his mind's eye, the boy he had lost, now a man caught up in his father's vendetta. Was this really the legacy he wanted to leave? Was revenge worth the cost of dragging Aaron down with him?

Walter pushed the doubts aside. Harold Gardner had taken everything from him. It was only fair that Walter returned the favor. And if he could find some twisted sense of closure in the process, so be it.

Walter's thoughts mulled over his clumsy, foiled attempts to exact revenge on Harold Gardner. He had to try again, if not Harold, then those he held dear. His hands performed the routine tasks as his mind continued to plot.

As the last of the passengers filed off the ferry, Walter turned back to his duties, a grim determination etched into his features. He'd be on a layover on the island tomorrow. The game was afoot, and he was ready for his next move.

Chapter Fourteen

On the Hook

The tang of the lake air filled Doug's lungs as the *Sandpiper*, a 38-foot charter fishing boat, cut through the gently rolling waves off the coast of South Bass Island. Equipped with a flying bridge and a spacious stern for anglers, the boat swayed slightly as it settled into position. The hum of the engine quieted, replaced by the rhythmic slap of water against the hull and the cries of gulls circling above, their eyes keen for scraps.

Doug leaned on the gunwale, watching the seagulls dive and skim just above the surface. The sunlight glinted off the lake, throwing silver ripples across the water. To any casual observer, the scene was idyllic—a perfect morning for fishing. But Doug wasn't feeling it.

His father slapped a hand on Doug's back, breaking his son's brooding reverie. Harold was in his late sixties, his once-broad shoulders slightly stooped, but his energy was undiminished. Harold was decked out in an old fishing hat speckled with faded lures and a T-shirt that read "Reel Men Fish."

"What's wrong, son? You don't look like you're enjoying the fishing," Harold asked Doug as the men sat in the chartered fishing boat.

Ron and Chuck both wound their reels in then let the line back out as they trawled for the walleyes the captain had reported running in the lake.

"I feel like I'm wasting my time when I should be out investigating the murder or at least hunting for Kowalski, not sitting here fishing," Doug said. He held his rod in one hand, the limp line floating in the water.

"I thought a day on the lake with your friends might help you relax and focus on what needs to be done next. Guess I was wrong."

"I appreciate the thought, Dad, but it's just so frustrating not being able to really investigate a crime without any resources. Tony hasn't gotten back to me yet. I'm not even in my jurisdiction and if it wasn't for being a target, I shouldn't have any say in the matter at all. I suppose I should be grateful that Sgt. Drake is allowing me carte blanche in his case."

Doug forced a smile that didn't quite reach his eyes. He adjusted his ball cap and stared out at the horizon, his mind still back at the island winery where the chaos had started. The murder investigation had hit one roadblock after another, and Walter Kowalski, the man Doug believed was central to the whole mess, was still out there, taunting them with every move.

"Hard to relax when there's a killer running loose," Doug muttered, his fingers tightening around the edge of the railing.

Harold shook his head. "You've been running yourself ragged. If we're going to figure this out, you need to be sharp. And you can't be sharp if you're wound tighter than a drum."

Ron, a longtime friend of Doug, chuckled from where he was fiddling with his fishing tackle. "Listen to your dad, Doug. You'll catch more fish if you stop scaring them off with that ferocious look."

Chuck, the fourth member of their fishing party and a no-nonsense Texan with a quiet demeanor, nodded in agreement. "Besides, you don't want us to out-fish you, Sheriff. Think of the stories we'll tell back in Meadowood."

Doug snorted but said nothing as he pulled his line out of the water.

He moved to the bait station, where a bucket of minnows and another of wriggling night crawlers sat, their earthy, fishy scent mingling with the lake breeze. He picked up a worm, its cool, slimy body squirming against his fingers, and threaded it onto a hook.

The boat rocked gently as Harold cast his line into the water, the reel singing as the lure flew out into the depths. "There," Harold said with satisfaction. "Now, if I can't catch a fish, it won't be for lack of trying."

Doug rolled his shoulders and finally dropped his line over the side again. The water swallowed the hook with a soft plunk, and the line spooled out smoothly. The rhythm of the boat, the cries of the gulls, and the soft slap of the waves worked their way into Doug's frayed nerves.

For a few minutes, the men settled into a comfortable silence. Chuck and Ron traded stories about fishing trips gone wrong, their laughter rising over the soft hum of the boat's generator. Harold adjusted his hat and grinned at Doug.

"You remember the first time I brought you out here?" Harold asked. "You were no bigger than a minnow yourself."

Doug smiled faintly. "Yeah, I remember. You caught a walleye bigger than me, and I swore I'd outdo you someday."

"And you still haven't," Harold teased, his grin widening.

The low rumble of the *Miller Ferry* approaching from the west interrupted their conversation. The large, white ferry glided steadily across the water, its deck bustling with passengers enjoying the ride back to Port Clinton.

Ron leaned on the railing, waving at the ferry. "Looks like a full house," he remarked. "Two more days and we'll be on it."

Harold squinted at the ferry, shading his eyes with one hand. His jovial expression darkened, and he muttered something under his breath.

"What is it?" Doug asked, immediately alert.

Harold pointed to the ferry's open deck. "Look there, near the rail. Tell me that isn't Walter Kowalski."

Doug followed his father's gaze and felt his stomach drop. Sure enough, standing at the railing with a smug expression was Walter Kowalski. He wore a pair of seaman coveralls and a ball cap, his dark eyes scanned the water before locking onto Doug and Harold aboard the *Sandpiper*.

Doug's fists clenched at his sides. "That son of a—"

Before he could finish, Walter lifted a hand in a mock salute, his grin widening. The gesture was infuriating, a blatant reminder of Doug's current impotence. They had no jurisdiction out here, no way to stop the ferry, no way to get to Walter before he reached the mainland. He knew it and taunted them.

Harold growled low in his throat. "The nerve of that man."

Doug's jaw tightened as he watched the ferry glide past, its wake rocking the *Sandpiper*. The captain of their boat gave them a curious glance from the flying bridge, but Doug ignored him, his focus fixed on Walter until the ferry disappeared into the haze.

"He's daring us," Doug said, his voice low and seething.

Ron stepped closer, his brow furrowed. "What are you going to do?"

Doug shook his head, frustration boiling over. "There's nothing I *can* do right now. He knows it. That's why he's on that ferry, smirking like he's untouchable."

"Listen, now you know where he is. That's a good thing. Looks like he's working on the ferry, which means he'll be making that crossing again. He'll be back on the island in a couple hours," Chuck said in an even tone.

Harold laid a hand on Doug's shoulder, his grip firm. "We'll get him, son. One way or another. You just have to keep your head."

Doug nodded reluctantly, but the knot of tension in his chest refused to loosen. He felt trapped, just like the lines they were using to fish—cast out, but still tethered, unable to reel in what mattered most.

The men returned to their fishing, but the mood on the boat had shifted. Doug's focus was no longer on the lake or the possibility of catching walleye. His mind was back on the investigation, turning over every detail, every missed opportunity, every clue that might lead him to Walter.

The hours passed in strained silence, the occasional splash of a fish breaking the surface or the whirr of a reel the only sounds. Doug barely noticed when Chuck finally hauled in a respectable catch, or when Harold laughed and handed over a wriggling yellow perch for Ron to photograph.

"Fish on the dinner menu tonight!" bragged Chuck.

By the time they returned to the dock, Doug's nerves were raw. His frustration simmered just beneath the surface. He knew his Dad had meant well by bringing him out here, but the trip had only reminded him of how much work was left to do—and how much was still out of his control.

As they unloaded their gear and said their goodbyes to the boat captain, Harold pulled Doug aside. "You'll catch him," he said firmly. "You've got that Gardner determination, and it's going to pay off. Don't let him get in your head."

Doug nodded, though his expression remained grim. "Thanks, Dad. I just hope you're right."

Harold patted him on the back, his own frustration tempered by years of wisdom. "I'm always right. Now, go do what you do best—and don't let that smug punk get away with it. Meet you back at the condo."

Doug watched as his father walked toward one of the golf carts. Chuck climbed in next to Harold and piled their gear and ice chest filled with their catch into the back of the cart.

They left him standing at the edge of the dock. The lake stretched out before him, calm and vast, but it offered no solace.

Doug turned toward the other vehicle, determination hardening his features. Ron waited quietly for him. The friends nodded in silent communication.

Walter Kowalski might have slipped through his fingers today, but Doug wasn't about to let it happen again.

The hunt was far from over.

Chapter Fifteen

Close Call

We decided to spend a leisurely afternoon picnicking at the scenic South Bass Island State Park. The park, with its expansive meadows, towering white oaks, and spicy bay laurel was the perfect spot to unwind. A gentle breeze carried the sweet scent from the Jane Coates Wildflower Trail. Our group set up a picnic table near the edge of the park, where the view of Lake Erie was spectacular—sparkling waves lapping against the rocky shoreline. Our time on the island would end soon. We wanted to enjoy the solitude and island beauty.

Johnny, Billy, and their friend Stevie were brimming with energy. The idea of lounging around didn't appeal to them for long. "Can we rent bikes, Mom?" Johnny asked, his face lit with excitement.

Doug nodded before I could respond. "As long as you stick together and stay in the park," he said, handing Johnny a few bills for the rental. "You look after your brother too."

"Don't go too far, and check in every half hour," I added, unable to resist ruffling Billy's hair as he bolted off with his brother and Stevie.

We gals settled into our chairs, unpacking sandwiches and lemonade, while the men bragged about yesterday's fishing trip and who caught the largest fish. I couldn't help but feel a pang of nervousness as I watched the boys ride off. Chastising myself for being paranoid, I brushed it aside.

Ron and Colleen wandered off to explore the famous park wild-flower trail and hunt for butterflies. I think the newlyweds just wanted some time alone. Smiling, I watched them stroll off.

Unbeknownst to the family, Walter Kowalski had been watching them from a distance. Perched on a bench near the bike rental stand, his unassuming cap and sunglasses allowed him to blend into the park's relaxed atmosphere. He'd been following the boys since they mounted their bikes, his expression a mixture of anger and grim determination.

Walter's plan was simple yet cruel: target Doug Gardner's family to make Harold feel the same helplessness and loss Walter had endured. The boys, with their carefree laughter and innocence, were a painful reminder of the life Walter had lost. He couldn't hurt them physically—he wasn't entirely without a conscience—but he could scare them, send a message to their father and grandfather that they weren't untouchable.

The three boys paused on their bikes, catching their breaths, as they surveyed the trails ahead dividing into two directions. Johnny leaned across the bike handlebars, turning to his friend.

"Hey ... do you have any idea what's going on?" Stevie asked.

Johnny glanced toward his younger brother then bent his head closer to his friend. "I kind of listened to my dad and grandpop talking last night. I'm not sure I understand exactly what's going on, but they kept talking about some guy that wants to hurt us."

"Whoa, that's heavy. Who?"

"Dunno. I heard the name Walter, but I'm not sure if that's who they meant. I think my dad thinks this Walter might have poisoned the dude at the winery. Mom's worried but she's trying not to show it."

"Yeah, my mom and dad are trying to act cool, like nothing is wrong, but I heard them whispering too. Makes me think of that spooky guy during Halloween a couple years ago."

"Hey, what are you two talking about?" asked Billy as he scooted his bicycle closer to the older boys.

"Nothing. Let's race to the monument trail!" Johnny shouted, pedaling ahead of Billy and Stevie.

"I'm not losing to you!" Stevie yelled, pushing himself to go faster.

"Aww, c'mon Johnny, wait up!" cried Billy as he followed behind.

The boys didn't notice the man who had subtly altered his path to intersect with theirs. Walter had carefully timed his movements, ensuring that no other adults were near the trail.

As the boys sped around a bend, they suddenly found themselves confronted by a man who had fallen across the path, groaning dramatically. "Help! My ankle—I think it's broken!" Walter called, his voice strained.

The boys skidded to a stop. "Should we get help?" Billy asked, looking uncertainly at his brother.

"I don't know. Maybe we can help him up?" Johnny replied, already stepping off his bike.

Stevie hesitated, glancing nervously back down the trail. "Guys, this feels weird. We should get your dad."

Walter groaned louder, clutching his ankle. "Please, just help me stand. I'll be fine—I just need a hand."

Both older boys looked at the stricken man.

Sitting at the picnic site, I couldn't shake a sense of foreboding. I got up and began to pace. I had checked my watch twice already, noting that the boys had been gone longer than I liked.

"Doug," I said, my voice tinged with worry, "the boys haven't come back to check in yet. Something's wrong. It's been awhile."

Doug glanced up from his plate. "They're probably just having fun. I'll give them a few more minutes before we go looking."

Maude, sitting nearby with her ever-watchful gaze, frowned. "I agree with Merry. It's not like the boys to ignore the rules."

"All right, if it will relieve your mind," Doug said.

"Let's split up and look," I insisted, stopping my pacing.

Anna read my worried expression and jumped up to join me. "Stevie knows the rules. This isn't like him either. I'm coming. C'mon Chuck!"

Our group quickly formed search pairs—Doug and Harold took the main trail, Maude and I headed toward the monument, while Anna and Chuck moved toward the picnic area's perimeter. Ron and Colleen hiked toward the rocky cliffs near the water's edge.

Maude and I picked up our pace as we climbed the path toward Perry's Monument. We both called out the boy's names as we searched the trail.

"They'll be okay," Maude said, trying to stay calm.

"Do you think Kowalski has done something?"

"No. Didn't Doug and Harold say they saw him on the ferry heading back toward Port Clinton? He's not on the island."

"That was yesterday. What if he's returned?"

Back on the trail, Stevie was kneeling beside Walter, attempting to help him up, when Johnny's instincts kicked in. He recalled his father's law enforcement training and warnings. "Wait!" he shouted, pulling Stevie back just as Walter reached for his arm.

"What are you doing?" Stevie exclaimed.

Johnny pointed to Walter's other hand, hidden beneath his jacket, which was gripping a small canister of pepper spray. "He's not hurt! Run!"

The boys jumped on their bikes and pedaled furiously; their hearts pounded. Walter rose to his feet, cursed, and started running after them.

Maude and I had just reached the trail's entrance when we saw the boys barreling toward us, their faces pale and frantic.

"Mom! Grandma! A man—he tried to grab us!" Johnny shouted, skidding to a halt.

"He's after us," cried Billy.

I huddled the boys behind me. I'd use my body as a shield to protect them if need be.

My eyes widened as Maude sprang into action, stepping into the middle of the trail with surprising agility for her age. She fearlessly approached the charging man coming around the curve.

"Stop right there!" she bellowed, her voice commanding. She stood in the middle of the path like a pillar of stone, defying the oncoming man.

Walter froze, clearly not expecting to face an older woman blocking his escape route. He turned and darted into the thick underbrush and stand of trees, disappearing into the dense foliage.

"Help!" I shouted, hoping my voice would be heard over the wind.

Doug and Harold arrived moments later. We pointed toward the trees. Doug rushed toward the dense forest. I heard him crashing through the undergrowth, but he was too late.

"What happened?" Doug asked as he slowly joined us where we crouched together, hugging the boys and calming our own shaking nerves.

"It was Walter Kowalski," Maude stated. "He chased the boys and when I confronted him he fled like the coward I always knew he was."

"Are you sure? He can't have gone far. Maybe we can still catch him if we spread out," Doug said as he dragged his hand through his hair and looking around wildly. He stood and listened for sounds of Walter's retreat but the park was quiet except for the sounds of water lapping on the shore and the birds overhead.

Harold helped Billy push his bike back down the trail while clasping the youngster's hand protectively. Following behind him, I had Johnny and Stevie in tow. I noticed the slump of Harold's shoulders and knew he felt responsible for causing his family to be in danger. Doug was so like his father; I witnessed the same expression on his face.

Our group reconvened at the park's ranger station, where we each gave a statement to the authorities detailing the kidnapping attempt and the identity of the man we believed behind it. The boys, though shaken, were unharmed. Stevie and Johnny both received endless praise for their quick thinking in the situation. The ranger promised to notify the Put-in-Bay police station and Sergeant Drake.

As we returned to our picnic site, the tension slowly eased. Anna quipped, "Well, I didn't think our outing would include a foot chase. But at least we got our daily count of steps in."

Johnny wrapped his grandmother in a hug. "You're a super hero, Grandmom."

"Yeah, just like Wonder Woman," added Billy with a grin.

Anna couldn't help but laugh, despite the day's chaos. "You're a force to be reckoned with, Maude."

Doug placed a reassuring hand on my shoulder. "You were right to trust your instincts. Walter underestimated all of us, especially you."

As the sun dipped lower on the horizon, painting the lake in shades of gold and amber, we realized how lucky we had been. Our children's safety was all that mattered. They'd had a close call and one we all were extremely thankful turned out as it did.

The danger wasn't over. This time we had defeated Walter Kowalski's scheme. Until the next time.

Chapter Sixteen

Teapots and Trouble

The village possessed the kind of postcard charm that begged for a second visit. We drove Anna's golf cart into town and parked along the same side street Maude had used. Narrow streets lined with weathered buildings seemed to lean into each other like old friends. Flower boxes overflowed with petunias, and the smell of fresh-baked bread wafted from the bakery down the block. South Bass Island was the perfect blend of nostalgia and quirk, and while I loved the peace of my tea shop and Meadowood home, this place came in a close second.

Anna walked beside me, her sandals slapping against the cobblestones as she tilted her cowgirl hat to shade her eyes. "You sure about this, Merry? You already bought two tea sets yesterday."

"Yes, Anna. I'm sure. It's not every day you find vintage teapots that don't cost an arm and a leg," I replied, scanning the row of shops.

"Well, sugar, if you think we can sell them for a profit, let's go for it."

I laughed, "I know the shop's shelving is groaning under the weight of my finds, but these are so pretty. I'm sure they'll be popular."

The antique store's door jingled as we stepped inside. The scent of lemon polish and the faint mustiness of old books greeted us. Light filtered through lace curtains, casting intricate patterns on wooden displays. Every surface was crammed with treasures—delicate china, vintage jewelry, and oddities like an antique birdcage fit for an exotic parrot.

"Look at this," Anna said, holding up a silver sugar bowl shaped like a pumpkin. "Our teapots could use some company."

"Don't tempt me. It's darling. I like the pumpkin design," I replied, heading to the back where I'd spotted the tea sets the day before. "How much is it?"

Anna turned the silver bowl upside down and read the price sticker. "Whoa ... it's not that cute. Wow, for this price, we could buy ten of those teapots."

"Uh oh. Better put it back then," I said as I continued my search among the dishes displayed.

We spent the next fifteen minutes debating the merits of floral patterns versus geometric ones. I was just about to take a picture of a particularly dainty set to send to my Aunt, when Anna nudged me. "Merry, don't look now, but guess who's at the bar across the street?"

Curiosity got the better of me. I turned, peering through the shop's lace-curtained window. Sitting at an outdoor table at The Rusty Anchor was John Parker, the man who had been spying on us at the condo and seemed connected to the chaos that had been unraveling our vacation.

"Well, well," I murmured, slipping my phone into my pocket. "I think it's time we had a chat with Mr. Parker."

Anna grinned. "Now, this is more fun than antique shopping. I'd like to get my hands on that man."

The Rusty Anchor was a hodgepodge of nautical décor—life preservers on the walls, a ship's wheel behind the bar, and fishing nets draped across the ceiling. Only two customers sat on barstools, but only one interested us. The place appeared almost empty this early in the day. Parker nursed a beer and fiddled with a cocktail napkin. His hunched posture made him look like a man with the weight of the world on his shoulders.

"Mr. Parker," I said, stepping up to his table with Anna flanking me.

His head snapped up, eyes darting between us. "What do you want?"

"To talk," I said, sliding onto a stool without waiting for an invitation. Anna leaned against the bar rail, arms crossed like a bouncer who wasn't afraid to toss him out.

"Talk about what?" Parker asked, his voice gruff.

"Oh, I don't know," I said lightly, "maybe about how you ended up with a key from Maurice to Mr. Dobkin's condo. Or how you just happened to be lurking around and following my family. I saw the photos you took too."

He blanched, and I leaned in. "And how you're connected to Walter Kowalski."

At the mention of Kowalski, Parker's hand trembled, nearly spilling his beer. "I don't know what you're talking about."

Anna snorted. "Sure you do. Think hard. Because normal people don't carry out covert missions spying on people."

"You don't understand," Parker said, glancing nervously toward the bar.

"Then enlighten us," I said. "Because right now, you're looking like an accessory to murder. My husband would love to have a chat with you down at the police station."

Parker's face turned ashen. "Walter dragged me into this. I didn't have a choice."

"Of course you didn't, you're an innocent man" Anna said sarcastically. "More likely, you're a con man involved in a scam."

Parker scowled but didn't deny it. "I knew Walter from some ... jobs we pulled together years ago. He heard I was on the island and contacted me. Said he had a score to settle."

"With the Gardners," I said flatly.

He nodded reluctantly. "I didn't know the entire plan. I swear.

Walter told me to keep tabs on you, said he'd take care of the rest. I didn't know someone was going to get hurt."

"Nice try," Anna said, her voice hard. "But your story doesn't explain why you showed up at the condo a full week before we arrived."

Parker's eyes darted around, his breathing quickening. "Look, I came onto the island trying to earn a few bucks. Like you said, I had a con planned—didn't have anything to do with you folks. I got a call the morning you arrived, a chance to earn some extra cash taking pictures. I uh ... I was just doing what I was told."

"Not good enough," I said, pulling out my phone. "I'm calling Doug."

Parker shot out of his chair so fast that it tipped over. "I'm not going to jail!" he shouted, shoving past me. I bounced into the edge of the bar, barely staying upright.

"Stop him!" Anna yelled.

I grabbed for his arm but missed, and Parker bolted for the door. Anna lunged after him, but he twisted away, sending her stumbling into a table. I tried to follow, my heart pounding, but Parker was already out the door and disappeared down the street. Concerned for Anna, I knelt next to her to check on her injuries.

"Are you okay?" I asked Anna, helping her up.

"I've had gentler dances at a honky-tonk," she said, brushing herself off. "Let's talk to the bartender."

The man behind the bar was a burly guy with a thick beard and a "Don't Mess with Texas" T-shirt. He looked up as we approached, his eyes wary.

"Hey Tex, did you see where that guy went?" I asked, nodding toward the door.

"Nope," he said, wiping a glass. "And I'm not looking to get involved."

"Oh, you're already involved," Anna said sweetly, leaning on the bar. "Unless you want us to tell the police you're obstructing an investigation."

The bartender snorted. "You broads don't look like cops, but his name's John Parker."

"We know his name. I asked where he went," I repeated. Facing the bartender, my hands on hips, I glared at the man until he shifted his stance and looked down at the floor.

"He's been coming here for a couple of weeks, pays cash and keeps to himself. What he does when he leaves here, I don't care or need to know. Talked about staying at the Blue Horizon Motel on the edge of town."

"Did he ever meet with Walter Kowalski?" I asked.

The bartender frowned. "I don't know the man, but Parker may have mentioned him once. He clammed up quick, like he wasn't supposed to say the name. Look, that's all I know."

Anna gave him a pointed look. "You better hope you're telling the truth."

As we left the bar, I pulled out my phone to try Doug again, but it went straight to voicemail. "We need to get to that motel," I said, my determination outweighing the growing ache in my bruised elbow.

"Are you sure we should do that by ourselves? Don't you think you should wait for Doug?"

"What harm can it do? We're just going to confirm where to find Parker. We've already talked with him. I don't want the man jumping on the next boat off this island and disappearing for good."

"Okay, if you say so. At least we got some answers out of him. We've got an explanation of how he came to be in that condo a full week before we even arrived," Anna said.

"Yeah. I think he told the truth. I'm wondering if Walter somehow knew our names from the ferry boat. Maybe on our tickets or something? He had to know who we were when we arrived at the island then got hold of his friend. It's the only thing that makes sense."

We returned to the shop and retrieved our purchases, thanked the clerk for minding them, then headed to the golf cart. Placing the bags on the floor in the back, Anna looked at me and chuckled.

"Where to? Do we even know where we're going?"

I pulled my phone out and typed in the name Blue Horizon Motel into the *Waze* app. The name popped up with an address and directions.

"Okay. Head down this street then turn left toward the docks. According to this map, doesn't look that far away."

"Okey dokey. Here we go," Anna said as she drove the electric vehicle through the village streets.

As we neared the marina and docks, I pointed out a weathered blue clapboard structure with a crooked sign hanging on a pole. The chipped paint read Blue Horizon Motel. We drove into the parking lot of the motel and found a newer sign nailed to the entrance in bright red letters proclaiming the motel permanently closed.

"Well, I'll be! That scoundrel at the bar lied to us," Anna exclaimed.

"Guess this was a dead end. Let's go back to the condo and see what news the guys have."

Chapter Seventeen

Revelations

Anna and I entered the lobby of our condo complex. Amelia waved from the front desk.

"Hello ladies!" Amelia greeted us. "We'll miss having you here after you leave for home tomorrow."

"Thanks Amelia. How's the new job doing?" I asked.

"Just fine. Busy, but I'm managing."

"I'm sure you are. Have a good day."

We stepped into the elevator and pushed the button for the seventh floor.

"Nobody is going to sneak past that little gal," commented Anna.

"I think you're right, not with Amelia on the rental desk."

We parted as we left the elevator. Anna walked to her unit, and I turned to mine. Juggling my purse and shopping bag, I reached for the doorknob. Billy yanked the door open before I had a chance to turn the knob. I stumbled and almost fell into the room.

"Sorry Mom. I heard you in the hall and thought I'd help."

"Mm-hmm, I appreciate it. Just didn't expect to be thrown off balance. What are you guys up to?"

"We're going down to the pool for a while. Grandmom said we

could watch fireworks later," Billy said as he picked up his towel. I noticed he had a bag of chips and a can of soda tucked under his arm.

"I hope you guys aren't filling up on a bunch of junk food." I raised my eyebrow and shot him a look of reproach. He squirmed under my pointed stare.

"Aww Mom, we're on vacation. Just this once ... please?"

"All right, but you better eat your dinner tonight. Be careful," I said as Johnny joined his brother and headed out the door to meet Stevie. "Stay on our property."

Harold and Maude sat on the balcony drinking tall glasses of iced tea. They came inside when they saw me in the kitchen.

"Looks like you've been shopping," Harold commented, pointing to the large bag.

"Get everything you wanted?" asked Maude.

"Mm, yeah, I found another lovely tea pot and a set of cups and saucers that will match the floral pot I bought the other day. Our customers love using the delicate tea sets and they sell like hot cakes. I'm always replacing our inventory."

I carried my packages to our room then returned to the kitchen.

"Where's Doug? I tried calling him but it went to his voice mail. It's not like him to remain incommunicado."

"He received a message from that deputy in Meadowood. Tony? Seemed to rile him. Next thing I knew, he took the golf cart and rode into town to speak with Sgt. Drake," Harold said.

"Hmm, wonder what Tony sent him? Would you believe, Anna and I had a run in with our resident con man, John Parker, at a bar across from that antique shop?"

Maude gasped at that bit of news. "Oh my goodness."

"That's why I was calling Doug. According to Parker, he was on the island working some scam a week before we arrived and Kowalski tracked him down. It was Walter who put him up to tailing us. Guess it was just a lucky coincidence that Parker was squatting in the same complex. Gave him the perfect location to spy on us."

"Where's that vile man now?" asked Maude.

"I don't know. Anna and I chased him but he disappeared. The bartender told us a bogus address for some motel where he claimed Parker was staying, but when we drove there, the place was closed. So that was a dead end."

"It isn't safe for you to be running around this island investigating on your own." Harold scolded me, sounding just like his son. "You women could have been injured."

Sheez! Now I had two of them telling me what to do.

The words on the computer message kept repeating in my mind. I couldn't believe it, yet part of me knew it made sense. Even Dad told how Walter Kowalski's wife had left him and took her two children to start a new life. Punching in Tony's number, I needed to speak to him direct. I leaned back in the creaky wooden chair of the Put-in-Bay police station lobby, holding the phone to my ear as Tony's words sank in.

"Doug," Tony said, his voice low and urgent, "it's confirmed. Kowalski's son Aaron changed his last name to Drake when his mother divorced. It's her maiden name. Put two and two together, and I'd bet the farm, your buddy Sergeant Drake is Walter Kowalski's boy."

I clenched the phone tighter. "Thanks, Tony. I owe you."

"You owe me a beer," he quipped, then grew serious. "Doug, be careful. If Drake's been helping his father, this could go south fast."

I hung up and stared at the station's bulletin board plastered with ferry schedules, lost dog notices, and a faded map of the island. My gut churned. Drake had been nothing but professional since we'd arrived. Pretending to be the nervous kid wanting to do good, maybe too good, now that I thought about it. And if he'd been feeding Walter Kowalski information, that meant my family's safety had been compromised from the start. I felt like such a fool for buying his act.

The door to Drake's office was ajar, and I could see him at his desk, his posture rigid as he typed something into his computer. I knocked once and stepped in before he could respond.

"Sheriff Gardner," he said, standing up and moving toward me. "What can I do for you?"

"Close the door, Sergeant," I said, keeping my tone steady.

His brow furrowed, but he did as I asked. The door clicked. Drake slowly moved behind his desk. I watched him slide his hand toward an upper drawer, pause, then placed his palm flat on the desktop.

"We need to talk," I said, sitting down across from him. "About your father, Walter Kowalski."

Drake froze, his hand lingered on the edge of his desk. For a moment, the only sound was the hum of the fluorescent light overhead.

"I don't know what you mean," he said carefully.

"Oh, I think you do," I replied, leaning forward. "You see, my deputy back home did some digging. Turns out Walter Kowalski had a son named Aaron Drake Kowalski. A son who changed his last name to Drake and became a cop in Put-in-Bay."

Drake's jaw tightened. "This is ridiculous."

"Is it? Don't play dumb," I shot back. "Walter's been targeting my family since the moment we set foot on this island. And you've been conveniently close by the whole time. Coincidence? I couldn't figure out how he knew about our activities on the island. Between Parker keeping tabs and me foolishly calling you whenever we had some outing planned, Walter could pick and choose his time to strike."

He didn't answer, but his eyes darted to the door.

"Don't bother," I said. "You're not walking out of here until we clear this up."

Drake sank back into his chair, his shoulders slumping. "Fine. Yes, Walter's my father. I haven't seen him in years. He contacted me. I didn't ask to be dragged into this."

"No one's accusing you of more," I said. "But you sat back and let him wreak havoc. You helped him, didn't you? What'd he promise you, Drake? Money? A way to clear his name?"

He shook his head, his expression pained. "It wasn't like that. He showed up out of the blue, said he needed my help. Pleaded. Said it was his last chance to make things right."

I snorted. "And you believed him?"

Drake's voice rose. "He's my father, okay? You don't know what it's like—growing up with nothing, hearing everyone whisper about how your dad's a criminal. I thought maybe ... maybe I could help him turn things around."

"And instead, you became an accessory," I said bluntly.

Drake winced. "I didn't know how far he'd go. He said he just wanted information. I didn't think—"

"You didn't think he'd poison someone? Tamper with a golf cart? Threaten my family?" My voice echoed in the small office.

Drake buried his face in his hands. "I didn't know about the poison or the brakes until it was too late. I swear. I tried to stop him after that."

"But you know now," I said, my tone sharp. "Make this right or you're going down with him. If you have any decency left, you'll tell me where he is."

Drake looked up, his eyes filled with torment. "I can't."

"You can't or you won't?"

"He's my father," he said again, his voice cracking.

"And my family is at risk on this island because of him!" I snapped. "If you don't help me stop him, you're as guilty as he is."

Drake stood abruptly, pacing the room. "You don't understand. He lost everything because of your father—his job, his wife, his children! He didn't deserve it! If I betray him now, he'll—"

"You think Harold made your father drink himself into oblivion? Made him steal from the business they shared? Your dad destroyed his own life, Drake. My parents were victims of your father's deceit and my wife and children had nothing to do with it."

Drake's face twisted in anger. "That's not how he sees it! And after everything he's been through, I'm not going to stand by and let him suffer alone."

"Helping him isn't going to fix the past," Doug said. "It's only going to ruin your future. Do you want to end up like him?"

For a moment, Drake looked like he might lash out, but then his shoulders sagged. He fell forward across the desk, burying his face in his hands.

"I didn't want to hurt anyone," he said, his voice muffled. "I just ... I thought if I helped him, he'd finally forgive me for staying with my mom. For leaving him."

The station phone rang, cutting through the tension. Drake froze, his eyes flicking to it like it was a snake ready to strike.

I nodded to Drake. "Answer it. Put it on speaker."

"Help! This is Maude Gardner." Panic filled her voice. "Walter Kowalski was here. He's taken our boys. He says he'll—" She broke into sobs; her normal composure shattered.

"What? Mom! Tell me what happened," I demanded over the speaker phone, my blood turning to ice.

"Oh my God, Douglas! Is that you? Come quick. He hurt Amelia and Merry's taken off," she whispered.

The line went dead.

I stood, my fists clenched. "He has my sons. Drake, you can still make this right. Tell me where he is."

Drake's face turned white. His hands trembled as he turned to me and stuttered, "He ... he's hiding out in an old boathouse near the lighthouse. He said he wanted to scare you, but ... I think he's planning something worse. I didn't—"

"Save it," I growled. "You're coming with me."

Drake hesitated, then nodded, guilt etched across his face.

As we left the station, the weight of what lay ahead pressed down on me. Walter Kowalski had already destroyed his family. I wasn't about to let him destroy mine.

Chapter Eighteen

Lighthouse Showdown

"What did Doug say before he left? You said he heard from Tony? I'm going to check his tablet," I said as I ran into our bedroom and scooped up the mini-computer and carried it back to the kitchen.

"Can you access that thing?" asked Harold.

"I can as long as Doug hasn't changed his password. I, uh, sort of found his password one day and might have used it to snoop occasionally. For a good cause, of course." I gave my father-in-law a quick smile with a shrug of my shoulders.

I tapped in the alpha-numeric code and crossed my fingers until the image emerged and the tablet came alive. "Eureka!"

Scrolling through the text message from Tony to Doug, my fingers paused on the touchpad and my eyes widened as I read the name *Aaron Drake Kowalski*. It flashed across the screen of Doug's tablet, stark and undeniable. Walter's son.

"Jeez Louise! Look at this!"

Maude and Harold crowded next to me to read the screen.

A scanned newspaper clipping popped up in the file. It was a younger Drake—barely out of the academy—but unmistakably him.

The caption confirmed the connection: *"Son of Walter Kowalski, parolee, seeks a career in law enforcement."*

The room felt colder, the tension thick enough to cut. We had trusted this man. All this time ... he had tricked us. I recalled Drake's actions when he led Parker away at the Perry Monument and how quickly Parker had been released, only to follow us to the concert. It made sense now. They'd been working together. I stared at the screen, speechless.

A pounding on our door broke my stupor. I hurried to open it and found a terrified Anna standing in the hall. Her face flushed and her eyes wide; she grabbed my hands.

"That lunatic grabbed our boys! He shoved them into a rusty van just as I walked down to the pool. I heard the boys shouting and crying."

I dragged her into the apartment as my heart stopped then began to beat again. A chilling calm came over me as I swore to kill anyone endangering my sons.

"Was it Parker or Kowalski? Who has our boys?" I asked in an even, deadly tone.

"The older guy from the winery ... Kowalski."

"Okay, let's go get our boys. They can't get far. We're on a darn island, for Pete's sake." I turned to my father-in-law. "Think. Harold, where could he hide? You know the island. Where could he take them that's away from people? Some place isolated or private."

Harold sunk down onto a chair, his legs refusing to support him as his face turned ashen. He never thought his old partner would go so far as to harm children.

"Um, I dunno. Maybe the lighthouse. There's a rickety dock nearby plus an old boathouse that the village was planning to tear down. He could be there. It's a long shot."

"C'mon Anna. Get Chuck and let's go."

"Keep trying to call Doug. Phone the police station. Tell him what happened. We've got to go. Walter's already got a head start on us," I said.

I reached into my handbag and pocketed a canister of pepper spray. Rummaging through Johnny's backpack, I found his scout pocket knife and added that to my meager arsenal. Seeing Maude's new walking stick propped up in the kitchen's corner, I grabbed it for good measure as we dashed out of the condo.

Anna, Chuck, and I rushed into the lobby. Poor Amelia lay on the floor. A bloody gash on her head showed evidence of Walter's intrusion.

I picked up the phone and called Maude upstairs.

"Get an ambulance here. Amelia is hurt. She must have tried to stop Walter and got hit for her efforts."

We ran out of the building and jumped into a rented golf cart. I bemoaned the cute vehicle in a situation like this. I'd give anything to be behind the wheel of a real car. I missed my powerful SUV. We sped down the path toward a narrow village street that skirted the island coast and headed toward the lighthouse point. Chuck drove the cart like a mad man, pushing it to its limits in our haste to reach the boys. Anna and I clung to the sides of the cart, lest we tumbled out.

Demanding to drive, I slid behind the wheel of the police cruiser as Drake jumped in next to me and we raced toward the South Bass Island Lighthouse. We both sat silently, each absorbed in thought. My thoughts centered on capturing the man who held my children. He had committed murder once; he wouldn't shrink from doing it again. Drake's thoughts were probably on the choices he had made that would alter his life from this day forward. I hoped so. I hoped he wouldn't betray me when confronting his father.

As we approached the lighthouse, the secluded area looked eerily peaceful. The powerful Fresnel lens cast a beam across the expansive water, warning sailors of dangerous shoals but left the park grounds behind dark.

The towering structure cast a long shadow over the rocky shore, the sound of waves crashing against the rocks the only noise breaking the silence. I killed the car engine, and we stepped out cautiously. My hand caressed the smooth hilt of the revolver in my pants' pocket. I'd use it if I had to.

The wind off Lake Erie whipped around us, carrying the damp, briny scent of the freshwater and a chill in the air. A clattering sound made me spin around and grab for my gun. I couldn't believe my eyes as Merry, Anna, and Chuck came hurtling toward me. Their golf cart shook and rattled; a plume of smoke belched from under the frame. They skidded to a stop as the vehicle gave one last shudder and died.

"What are you doing here?" I demanded in a hoarse whisper.

"Walter kidnapped our boys. What do you think I'm doing here? I'm getting my sons, come hell or high water. That man doesn't know who he's dealing with ... he's gonna face two furious mothers ready to do battle," Merry said, her eyes sparking as she stood her ground.

Glancing at Anna, I recognized the same determination on her face. Walter definitely had poked the bear this time.

"All right, but you stay behind me and do as I say. He may have a gun and I don't think he'd hesitate to use it if cornered."

Merry approached Drake. She stared silently accusing him then suddenly drew back her right arm and landed a solid punch to the man's face.

"If anything happens to my boys, I will come after you. Do you understand me? Jail will be too good for you," Merry snarled.

Drake could only nod mutely as his hand cradled his cheek. I warned him before that my wife was a force to be reckoned with. Guess now he'd believe me.

"Let's spread out. Chuck, you and Anna search the boat house. Be careful. I doubt that structure is too stable. Merry and I are going to escort Sergeant Drake here into the lighthouse. Our kids have to be in one or the other of those places. If you see Kowalski, don't take any chances, shout out."

Chuck nodded and clasped Anna's hand as they started creeping toward the dilapidated boat house.

"Wait!" Merry called after them and ran up to Anna. She handed Anna the can of pepper spray and gave Chuck the folded scout knife. "You might need these. I've got Maude's handy bat," she said with a laugh. "Good luck." Merry hugged Anna fiercely, then ran back to where Drake and I stood.

"Ready?" I asked her as we crept toward the stone lighthouse.

The interior of the lighthouse was dimly lit, the faint glow of the last rays of sunlight filtered through the narrow windows. The air was cool and damp, carrying the faint metallic scent of rusted railings and weathered wood.

We moved cautiously up the spiral staircase, the creaking steps betraying every move. The light grew fainter the higher we climbed. I saw Doug draw his gun. He moved in a tense posture, like a lion ready to pounce. Drake followed, his shoulders hunched as if the weight of his father's actions pressed down on him. I crept silently behind them.

Straining to listen for sounds of the boys, my ears were only met with silence. Rhythmic slapping of lake waves against the shoreline and the gulls crying above could be heard. Where were they? Did that maniac hurt my sons? Were they lying somewhere crying for their mother? My mind spun. I had to take a deep breath to calm my fears and concentrate on the matter at hand.

At the top of the stairs, Walter Kowalski stood waiting. The small observation deck, enclosed by glass panels and low iron railings, offered no easy escape. Walter's wiry frame was silhouetted against the panoramic view of the lake and the darkening skies. His face wore a mask of cold fury. He stared at the approaching men.

"You brought him with you," Walter said, his gaze flicking between

Drake and Doug. He looked around the observation deck and rubbed his hands together like a greedy man counting his coins. "Didn't think you had it in you, son."

From my lower position, I could hardly make out Walter's form at the top of the darkened stairwell. Realizing that he hadn't discovered me further below on the stairs, I hung back in the shadows and clung to the wall.

Drake swallowed hard and stepped forward. "This ends here, Dad. Turn yourself in."

Walter laughed, a harsh, guttural sound that echoed through the confined space. "You think I'm just going to walk away? After everything they've taken from me?"

Doug moved near Drake, his gun trained on Walter. "Nobody took anything from you, Kowalski. Your choices put you here. You killed an innocent man. What of him?"

Walter's eyes darkened, his voice rising. "My choices? Harold Gardner destroyed me! He ruined my business, my reputation. My wife left me because of him. My son had to grow up without a father because of him!"

Drake's voice cracked as he spoke. "Mom left because of you, Dad. Your drinking, your lies. You did this to yourself."

Walter's hand shot out, grabbing a rusty crowbar from the floor. "Shut up! You don't get to lecture me, boy. You're just like them."

Doug's voice was calm but firm. "Put it down, Walter. Don't make this worse. You've hurt enough people."

Walter lunged toward Doug, swinging the crowbar wildly. Doug sidestepped just in time. The metal struck the railing with a deafening clang. I let out a gasp from the stairwell, my heart pounding as the fight unfolded above me on the upper deck.

Drake hesitated for a moment before stepping between them. "Dad, stop!" he shouted, grabbing Walter's arm.

Walter turned on him, his face a mixture of rage and disbelief. "You'd side with him over your own father?"

"I'm siding with what's right," Drake said, his voice steady despite the tremor in his hands.

Walter's eyes filled with a twisted mix of betrayal and heartbreak. "You're no son of mine."

Kowalski lashed out and struck Drake across his shoulders with the metal rod. The younger man screamed and fell backwards, tumbling down the spiral staircase, coming to rest a few feet below me.

I hurried down the couple of steps to where Drake lay twisted on the stairs. His leg was bent awkwardly under him while a large bruise ballooned on the back of his head where he'd hit the iron steps. He mumbled as I checked for signs of bleeding. I could do nothing for him right now. Deciding his injuries didn't appear life threatening, I left him and stealthily climbed the stairs again.

I listened to Doug trying to reason with Kowalski, in the same way trained police hostage negotiators speak in a soft reassuring voice. Kowalski was having none of it. As I crept higher, I saw Doug step closer, but Kowalski suddenly jumped backwards and pulled a gun from his back waist band.

Doug pointed his own revolver at the crazed man. "Put down your weapon, Walter. Don't do something you're going to regret."

Walter made a harsh laugh. "My entire life is a regret. You think you're so smart. You know nothing!"

My heart pounded in my chest as I heard the sounds of their scuffle on the observation deck. Shoes scraping the iron grates. Heavy breathing, grunts, and groans. A gun went skidding across the floor.

"Doug!" I called, my voice echoing against the stone walls.

"Merry, stay back!" Doug's voice carried down the stairs, strained and full of warning.

Like heck I'd stay back. My husband might have been the sheriff, but he was still my husband. I gripped Maude's walking stick, its polished oak weight reassuring in my hand, and gained the remaining narrow, twisting stairs. The iron was cold and slick from the damp air. I pressed against the stone wall to steady myself.

As I reached the top, the observation deck came fully into view—small, barely wide enough for two people to pass without bumping shoulders. The wrought-iron railing around the edge looked far too flimsy for comfort, given the sheer drop to the rocks below.

Doug and Walter engaged in a brutal struggle near the edge of the deck. Walter was taller and tough from working the boats, his face twisted in rage, but Doug's younger body strength and determination evened the odds.

"You ruined my life, Gardner!" Walter growled, trying to force Doug closer to the railing.

"You did that to yourself, Kowalski," Doug shot back, shoving him away with a grunt of effort.

Walter snarled and swung a fist at Doug, who scarcely dodged in time. The momentum sent Walter stumbling against the railing, and for one horrifying moment, I thought he might go over.

But Walter recovered, pointing his gun menacingly. The metallic glint caught the last rays of sunlight as he leveled it at Doug.

"I'm in charge now!" he barked, his voice trembling with rage. "You and your family took everything from me. Now you're gonna feel what that's like."

I froze, my breath catching in my throat. Doug slowly raised his hands; his eyes locked on Walter.

"Think about what you're doing," Doug said, his voice calm despite the situation. "It's over, Walter. You can still walk away from this."

Walter laughed bitterly. "This isn't over. I say when it's over. I'm not walking away and going back to prison."

He pulled the trigger.

The gunshot echoed, deafening in the confined space. The bullet ricocheted off the iron stairs with a sharp *ping* before embedding itself in Doug's upper arm. Doug cried out, staggered backward, and clutched his arm as blood seeped through his fingers.

"Doug!" I screamed, surging forward. My voice echoed off the stone walls.

My scream startled Walter. He pivoted toward me, his gun raised, but before he could fire again, I swung the walking stick with all my might. The heavy oak connected with his upper arm and shoulder, sending him spinning off balance. His gun clattered onto the iron grate flooring.

"You picked the wrong family to mess with, Walter!" I snapped, intending to swing the makeshift bat again.

He stumbled against the railing, regained his footing, then launched himself toward me. Hands extended like claws.

I swung Maude's walking stick with all my might and struck Walter on the back of his legs. His knees buckled and his footing faltered on the slick iron. Slipping, his arms flailed as he tumbled down the spiral staircase with a sickening series of thuds.

I rushed to Doug's side. Ripping a piece of cloth from my blouse, my hands shook as I pressed it against the wound on his arm. He was pale but still conscious, his jaw set in pain.

"Are you okay?" I asked, my voice trembling.

"I'll live," he said through gritted teeth. "Is he ...?"

We both looked toward the bottom of the staircase, where Walter's crumpled form lay motionless. Nearby, Sgt. Drake—Walter's son and accomplice—lay slumped against the wall.

Doug's face darkened. "Let's get out of here and see if Chuck and Anna have found our boys."

I helped him to his feet. Retrieving his and Walter's revolvers, and draping his good arm over my shoulder, we carefully descended the stairs. Siren sounds grew louder. Flashing lights of emergency vehicles illuminated the base of the lighthouse as they arrived on the scene. The sudden roar of a state police helicopter landing nearby surprised us. I breathed a partial sigh of relief, grateful to turn over the murderer to state law enforcement. However, I wouldn't feel whole and at ease until I found my children.

The officers rushed toward us, their guns drawn, but Doug waved them down after identifying himself. "Walter Kowalski's inside! And Sgt. Drake's on the stairs too! They both need medical attention."

They nodded, moving past us to secure the scene. One officer paused to offer us support, but Doug declined.

"We're fine," Doug said, though his wince told me otherwise.

As we exited the lighthouse, I exhaled a shaky breath, the tension finally lessening. Doug squeezed my hand, his gaze softening despite the blood staining his shirt.

"You did good, Merry," he said, his voice low. "I don't know what would've happened if you hadn't backed me up."

I managed a weak smile. "Told you we made a good team."

Doug pointed toward a tired motley crew walking toward us.

I gripped the cracked walking stick. "Oops, Maude's gonna need a new cane, but I'd say it was worth it."

"She won't mind. You're her favorite daughter-in-law."

I laughed. "I'm her only daughter-in-law."

Chapter Nineteen

Chuck's Boathouse Rescue

The wind whipped off Lake Erie, carrying the sharp tang of brine and decay as Anna Thompson tightened her scarf against the sudden chill. She glanced up at the silhouette of the South Bass Island lighthouse in the distance, its beam sweeping across the darkened shore. Somewhere ahead, her son Stevie and the Gardner boys, Johnny and Billy, were out there. Her heart clenched.

Chuck led the way along the uneven, rocky shoreline, the beam of his flashlight bouncing as he moved. He paused to examine the rotted wooden path stretching toward a boathouse that jutted precariously over the water.

"Anna," he called softly, waving her forward. "This place looks like it's about to collapse. You sure you're up for this?"

Anna placed her hands on her hips, narrowing her eyes at her husband. "Chuck Thompson, if you think I'm lettin' you go in there alone while our boy might be tied up inside, you've lost your ever-lovin' mind." Her Texas drawl softened the sharpness of her words, but the determination in her tone was unmistakable.

Chuck let out a resigned sigh, holding the flashlight steady as Anna joined him. "Just watch your step. These boards look like they've seen better days ... like around the time Roosevelt was in office."

The boathouse loomed ahead, a shadowy hulk against the restless lake. Its paint had long since peeled away, leaving the wooden siding weathered and gray. Several windows were shattered with jagged glass framing dark voids. Others hung crooked in broken frames. The roof sagged dangerously in places; rotten beams were exposed.

The waves of Lake Erie slapped rhythmically against the shore, their sound a harsh reminder of the isolation of the boathouse. A cool breeze carried the briny scent of algae and decaying wood, mingling with the faint cries of seagulls overhead.

As they stepped onto the deck, the boards groaned beneath their weight. Anna winced, glancing down at the dark water lapping just below the gaps in the planks. "Chuck, if this thing gives way, we're gonna end up wetter than a frog in a rainstorm."

He grunted, testing the next step with his boot. "We'll be fine. Just stick close."

"You keep that flashlight handy."

Waves slapped against the pilings. The old structure creaked and protested against the trespassers. A sudden rustling noise made Anna freeze, her heart leaping into her throat.

"What was that?" she whispered, gripping Chuck's arm.

He swung the flashlight toward the sound, revealing a rat scurrying across the deck and disappearing under a pile of debris. "Just a rat," he said, his voice steady. "We've faced worse than an oversized mouse. Let's keep moving."

Anna muttered under her breath, "If I wasn't so worried about Stevie, I'd be runnin' the other way right now. Stevie's in there. I can feel it. He has to be."

Chuck shone his flashlight on a gaping hole in the deck ahead.

"I'm mighty glad you brought that lamp; I'd be swimming right now if you hadn't shined that spotlight on that hole. We're gonna have to jump across it," Anna said in a shaky voice.

Chuck nodded, bracing himself and holding out a hand to steady her. "I'll go first."

With a short leap, he cleared the hole and turned to help Anna across. She hesitated for a moment, eyeing the dark water below, but Chuck's reassuring grip pulled her safely to the other side.

They reached the boathouse door, a warped and splintered piece of wood hanging crookedly on rusted hinges. Chuck pushed it open cautiously, the hinges protested with a loud screech.

Inside, the air was thick with the smell of mildew and rot. Damaged row boats, dinghies, and rusted gear were scattered across the floor casting long, ominous shadows in the flashlight's beam. Anna shivered. The darkness pressed in around them.

"Stevie?" Chuck called, his voice low but urgent. "Johnny? Billy? Are you boys in here?"

For a moment, there was only the sound of the waves and the faint creaking of the boathouse. Then, from the far corner, a faint noise.

"Mom? Dad?" Stevie's voice was barely audible, but it was enough to send Anna rushing forward.

"Over here!" another voice chimed in, followed by a chorus of whispers and muffled shuffling.

"Stevie! Where are you, baby?" she called, her voice catching in the back of her throat.

Chuck's flashlight illuminated a makeshift barricade of crates and broken oars. Three dirty faces peeked out from behind it, their eyes wide with fear.

"Thank the Lord," Anna whispered, her knees nearly giving out.

Chuck moved quickly, tossing aside the debris blocking the boys. As soon as the path was clear, Stevie bolted into Anna's arms, clinging to her as if his life depended on it.

"Mom!" he cried, his slender body trembling. "I was so scared."

Anna hugged him tightly, tears streaming down her face. "Oh, sweetheart, you're okay now. You're safe. Momma's got you."

Johnny and Billy scrambled out next, throwing themselves at Chuck, who caught them both in a tight embrace.

"Easy, boys," Chuck said, his voice thick with emotion. "You're okay now."

"Uncle Chuck!" Johnny sobbed. "He said he'd hurt our parents if we didn't do what he said."

Billy nodded, his voice shaking. "He made us get in the van. He said he'd come back and hurt us if we tried to run."

Chuck's jaw tightened, his free hand clenching into a fist. "That man's not gonna lay a finger on you boys again. I promise you that. Now, hold your arms out so I can cut that rope off you."

He began sawing the strands of rough rope that bound Billy's hands. Chuck moved over to Johnny, freeing his bound hands.

"Hey, is that my cub scout knife?" asked Johnny.

"Yeah, I think it is. Your mom gave it to me. Good thing, huh?"

Stevie pulled back just enough to look up at Anna, his face streaked with tears. "Mom, he said he was gonna hurt you and Dad. That's why we didn't try to get away."

Anna kissed his forehead, her voice gentle but firm. "You did the right thing, sugar. But he's not gonna hurt us, and he's not gonna hurt you or anyone. Not anymore."

Chuck finished removing the ropes from Stevie's hand and tossed the frayed cord aside.

The boys began talking all at once, their words tumbling over each other in a chaotic mix of fear and relief. Chuck held up a hand to calm them.

"Alright, alright," he said. "One at a time."

Stevie clung to Anna, his voice barely above a whisper. "He said we couldn't make any noise. He was so scary, Mom."

Chuck crouched down to meet the boys' eyes. "This man—Walter Kowalski—did he say what he planned to do?"

Johnny shook his head. "No. He just said we had to stay here until he came back."

Billy added, "He locked us in, but we pushed the crates to hide behind in case he came back."

Chuck nodded, his expression grim. "Smart thinking, boys. You boys are braver than most adults I know."

Anna stood, keeping Stevie close. "We need to get out of here. Doug and Merry are at the lighthouse—if anyone can catch Kowalski, it's them."

Suddenly, the distant sound of a gun shot echoed in the night. Anna and Chuck exchanged worried looks.

"Watch your steps. This dock is missing a few boards. I don't want to go fishing tonight if any of you guys fall in," Chuck said, trying to keep the mood light and calm their fears. "There's a big hole on the dock you're gonna have to jump over when I shine my flashlight on it. Okay?"

Chuck guided the group back toward the door. As they stepped onto the deck, the boathouse groaned ominously, but they moved quickly, their steps careful.

"Mom," Stevie whispered, his voice small. "What if he comes back?"

Anna squeezed his hand tightly. "He won't, baby. And even if he does, your daddy and Uncle Doug are gonna take care of him."

The night air felt colder as they reached solid ground, but the relief of having the boys safe made it easier to bear. Anna glanced at Chuck, her eyes filled with determination.

"Do you think Doug's caught up to him yet?" she asked.

Chuck shook his head. "If not, he's close. And when he does, Walter Kowalski's not gonna know what hit him."

"You got that right. I wouldn't give him a plug nickel if Merry gets her hands on him," Anna snorted. Her grip tightened on Stevie's hand as they made their way toward the lighthouse.

Chuck pulled out his phone. He frowned. "No signal."

. . .

As if in answer to his prayers, red lights flashed from above and the roar of a state police helicopter hovered overhead. Anna and the boys shielded their faces and took cover behind an overturned rowboat. The chopper blades kicked up dirt and debris as they landed in the open field. More emergency lights came into view as an ambulance barreled into the park and screeched to a halt near the lighthouse.

Merry and Doug stumbled out of the lighthouse as the officers and paramedics rushed inside. They leaned against each other, watching as the Ohio State troopers hauled Walter and Drake away in cuffs.

Merry held up her hand and waved to Chuck and Anna. They were a sight for sore eyes.

Billy and Johnny shouted to their parents ... music to Merry's ears. Her sons were safe. Merry took a deep breath and cried.

Her heart soared at the sight.

Billy and Johnny rushed toward her with arms open.

For the first time since this nightmare began, Merry felt the worse was finally over.

Chapter Twenty

Home, Sweet Home

Bedlam.

Voices filled the space as everyone talked, cried, and laughed simultaneously.

Maude and Harold embraced us. Maude cried unabashedly, tears running down her cheeks. Johnny and Billy even allowed her to smother them in hugs and kisses without objection for once. Harold fussed over Doug; his son's arm wrapped in a bandage and resting within a sling.

The room overflowed with happy people. I looked around at this group of wonderful, caring friends and family. We survived this nightmarish ordeal because of them. Colleen and Ron had taken charge, calling for emergency help and alerting the state police while we went in search of our boys.

A distraught Maude and Harold tried coping with the situation by tending to Amelia's head wound and alerting the condo complex residents to possible dangers from a returning Kowalski or Parker.

"Thank you!" I said, as I embraced Chuck and Anna again. "You saved my boys. There aren't sufficient words to thank you for your efforts. I'm just sorry that my invitation to share our vacation trip resulted in such a nightmare."

"Sugar, we're family. Families stick together and fight together. Isn't that right, Chuck?" Anna said as she snuggled within her husband's arms.

"That's right. I think our boys are the ones that deserve the recognition. They stayed calm, remembered their scout survival training, and faced the danger united," Chuck said.

"Yes, you're right. Our boys were all extremely brave."

Billy came to stand next to me. I couldn't resist drawing him into a hug and pressed a kiss on his cheek. He tolerated my display of affection.

"I'm hungry," Billy stated. "Grandmom said we could watch the fireworks tonight."

I laughed. "You mean you haven't had enough excitement for one day?"

"Yeah, but ... can we eat?"

"Hey everyone, let's go find some supper. How about a return to the Beer Barrel Saloon?" I suggested as I achieved everyone's attention.

"We may have to walk. Seems we're short one golf cart," Ron said with an accusing look toward Chuck. He couldn't keep the stern expression long before he burst out in laughter.

"And here I thought Merry was the only person who drove like a Nascar racer," Doug joined into the fun. "Chuck must have revved that cart up to fifty miles an hour before it blew."

Chuck's face flushed, sheepish, but his lips curled into a grin as he accepted the jibes.

We trooped down the few blocks into town and entered the Beer Barrel Saloon. The waiter directed us to the same large table we had occupied before.

"Welcome back," greeted the waiter.

"Thanks," I said, pleased that the server had remembered us.

He waited patiently then took our orders. Another server carried the tray of drinks to our table. She placed mugs of soft drinks and bottles of beer on the table then paused and stared at our group.

"Hey, aren't you the boys who were kidnapped? I heard all about it on the radio news. Gosh, you must be the hero that saved them," she said in awe as she stared at Chuck. "Can I shake your hand?"

Chuck turned beet red, mumbled something under his breath then held out his hand to the waitress.

"Um, thank you. It wasn't just me, but ..."

The owner of the restaurant hurried over to our table. He beamed as he slapped Chuck on the back and shook everyone's hands.

"Dinner is on the house, folks. It's the least we can do for real heroes. WKGB news out of Port Clinton broadcasted the entire story—how you solved the murder of that winery guide and saved your boys from kidnapping. I understand you had a big tussle at the lighthouse too. Wow! Sure wish they had pictures of that."

"Jeez Louise! We didn't know we made the news," I said.

"Are you kidding me? Sirens blaring all across the village and state police helicopters swooping in, that's a big deal. Reckon that's the most excitement our little island has had since the tall ships sailed into the harbor a couple years ago." He blurted out in one breath. "Too bad about that Sergeant Drake. Heard he got mixed up in it. How long you folks staying in Put-in-Bay?" the restaurateur asked, his voice dwindling as he paused to breathe.

"We leave tomorrow for home," Doug said quietly.

"Well, safe travels and I hope you all come back"

"Thanks," we replied, several voices speaking at once.

Harold grinned from ear to ear. "Our son, the celebrity. Let's toast to a happy ending." He raised his mug and we all clicked glasses.

"I insist you all come back to the island next summer for a more relaxing vacation. I feel we owe you all at least that much," Maude said as she reached across the table to squeeze the hands of Anna and Colleen then draped her arm across my shoulders in a brief hug.

Doug's cell phone rang. He glanced at the caller ID and took the call while everyone settled down, sipping drinks, and waiting on our meals.

I watched his as he listened to the caller and heard him make short noncommittal grunts.

"Who was that?" I asked as he ended the call.

"Trooper Thomas from Port Clinton. They picked up John Parker boarding the ferry. He's in custody for his part in assisting Kowalski."

"Good. So that's it then. He won't be bothering us or your parents again."

We were a more somber group as we sailed away from the island to retrieve our cars in Port Clinton and drive south to Meadowood. I made a sigh of relief as we finally entered Meadowood's main street. Colleen and Anna beeped their horns as they peeled off and turned toward their own homes. When we pulled into our driveway, our home never looked so good. I had phoned Aunt Fran during the drive back; she sat waiting on us with Mittens.

As soon as we exited the car, Mittens wiggled out of Fran's arms then nonchalantly strolled toward us. Being a cat, he dared not appear too excited to see his family again. Billy picked up the tabby and nuzzled the top of his head. I could hear the loud purrs from where I stood.

We straggled into the kitchen, dragging luggage behind us.

"So, did you all have a good vacation or did you die of boredom on that sand pile?" Aunt Fran asked as she embraced me in a welcoming hug.

"If you only knew!"

Also By: Nancy M. Wade

A Meadowood Mystery

•Scarecrows and Corpses

•Reunion With Death

•Deadly Bones

•Deathly Wedding Woes

•Berry Little Murder

•Deadly Secrets

A Maddie Brooke Mystery

•Innvitation to Murder

•Mysteries Beneath the Inn

Circle-D Saga Trilogy

•Endless Circle

•Moment In Time

•Gun For Hire

Author Biography

Now an award winning author, Nancy M. Wade challenged herself to finish the novel that had been started years earlier after she retired from the Dept. of Defense in 2012. The result one year later was "Endless Circle: A Circle D Saga".

Nancy and her husband are living their retirement dream in the hills of N.E. Tennessee. She's an active member of the Lost State Writer's Guild of the Tri-Cities area of TN/VA. Determined to complete another personal challenge and bucket list item, Nancy went back to school at the golden age of 69 to complete her bachelor's degree. Graduating in 2022 with Summa Cum Laude honors from East State Tennessee University, Nancy concentrated in criminology and film studies.

An avid lover of western movies and books, Nancy developed the *Circle-D Saga* — a western action adventure tale of love and hatred. The story begins in 1885 in "Endless Circle" with generations of three families: the Dunlap, Logan, and Hartman families. The saga follows the families during WWII in "Moment in Time" and the 3rd book in the trilogy called "Gun for Hire" tells the tale of gunslinger Cody Jarvis and his connection to the dynasty.

Based upon her years of living in the mid-west, Nancy wrote a small town, cozy mystery series: *A Meadowood Mystery* that showcases the antics of amateur sleuth housewife, Meredith Gardner, with "Scarecrows and Corpses", then added her adventures in "Reunion with Death", "Deadly Bones", "Deathly Wedding Woes", "Deadly Secrets", and the holiday tale "Berry Little Murder".

Nancy's latest cozy mystery series is ***A Maddie Brooke Mystery*** with "Innvitation to Murder", and "Mysteries Beneath the Inn"– a ghostly cozy murder mystery set in the Magnolia Blossom Inn, a historic southern bed and breakfast inn.

She is also the author of a rich family drama, ***Reflections: A Sentimental Journey,*** inspired by the courtship and early married years of her parents; a colonial historical romance novel, ***Frontier Heart***; and a contemporary short story called ***Courtship of Laura.***

Excerpt: "Deadly Secrets"

I t's summertime and the town of Meadowood is ready to party.

Meredith Gardner is in the thick of things again when Aunt Fran runs for town mayor and her opponent winds up dead!

Historic Meadowood is abuzz with excitement as it celebrates its bicentennial with a grand parade. Amidst the colorful banners, lively tunes from the high school band, and cheerful spectators, Scout leader Meredith Gardner tries to keep her troop in line. The atmosphere is festive, and the community is united in joy. But the celebration takes a dark turn when Mayor Dickson is found dead in his vintage red Cadillac, a small bloody hole marring his pristine white shirt.

As shock ripples through town, Merry's husband, Sheriff Doug Gardner, takes over the case. Together, they must untangle the web of secrets and hidden animosities that lie beneath Meadowood's idyllic facade. With suspects ranging from political rivals to disgruntled citizens, Merry uncovers the truth behind a plot that would be catastrophic for small-town Meadowood.

Merry and Colleen dig deep into the town's history and find a secret fraternal organization determined to wreak havoc on the community in a get rich scheme promoted in land owned by a limited liability company. The townsfolk will be shocked when the real owners of the company become known.

"Deadly Secrets" is a cozy mystery filled with charm, a tight-knit community, and a determined couple who won't rest until justice is served. Join Meredith, Doug, and Merry's gal pals as they navigate the twists and turns of this captivating whodunit, proving that even the quaintest towns can harbor the darkest, deadliest secrets.

Read **Chapter 1 — "Committee"** in the pages below.

Deadly Secrets: Chapter 1
Committee

Sneaking a look at the clock, I tapped my foot as I watched our last customer finish her tea and scones, then browse among the delicate tea cup sets and crocheted cozies before coming to the counter to check out. I was getting antsy.

"Thank you for coming. I hope you enjoyed yourself. I know you'll love using that adorable cozy at home; it's perfect for keeping your teapot warm," I said with a smile and handed the woman her bagged cozy and receipt as I hastened her to the door.

"I can't wait to show it to my friend Miriam. We'll be back," she enthused as she exited the tea shop. The bell over the door jingled as she left.

A glance at the clock on the wall confirmed it—two o'clock, closing time. Finally. It had been a hectic morning.

"Set the lock and flip the closed sign before anyone else pops in," said Anna. She cleared the small table. Juggling cups and plates in one hand, she headed to the kitchen.

I did as Anna suggested, then finished clearing the remaining tables and wiped them all clean. With a quick look around our quaint tea shop, I assured myself we were ready for the campaign committee meeting starting in the next half-hour.

There were days when I almost pinched myself, not believing this wonderful place was really mine, at least fifty percent of it. My dream had come true the day Anna Thompson had agreed to go into business with me and we purchased the shop. Anna and I had been instant friends from the time she and her husband Chuck moved into the area from Texas about six years ago. Anna's quirky sense of humor and homespun common sense conquered most situations. The fact that she had a son Stevie, born during her change of life, kept her young. Plus it gave us something in common since our sons were the same age, despite Anna being close to twenty years my senior. Anna was a tireless worker; I only prayed I had her stamina when I got to be her age.

We named our venture the A&M Tea Shop. For the past year, we had devoted all our energy to growing and marketing our enterprise, and now the quaint tea shop was a popular tourist attraction in Meadowood.

Our Victorian English tea shop contained small bistro tables with white linen tablecloths, adorned with tiny bud vases; they sat two or three guests comfortably. We served a variety of flavorful teas using delicate porcelain tea sets and miniature tea pots. The local bakery, Martha's Delites, was owned by a dear friend, Martha Parker, and provided delicious scones for our customers. We supplemented our baked offerings with muffins and cookies that Anna and I baked in the shop's kitchen. The addition of various petite tea sandwiches completed our daily menu. The atmosphere of the shop was restful and rather feminine with its graceful chintz upholstery and curtains. Decorative floral grapevine wreaths hung on the walls. Display cases filled with knit tea cozies, delicate demitasse teacups, and a collection of sugar bowls and creamers added to our customer's interest and boosted our sales.

Anna filled the tea kettles and started a fresh pot of coffee as I arranged an assortment of pastries from Martha's bakery onto a two-tiered tray. I placed several coffee mugs on the counter, ready for our expected guests.

"Everyone should arrive soon," Anna commented as she poured cold milk into a creamer and set it next to the sugar bowl.

"We're ready. I'll go check the door."

Leaving the kitchen, I walked to the front entrance and took up my watch post. I spotted Colleen and Aunt Fran coming down the walk. Two of my friends and cub scout mothers, Barb Williams and Carol Goodwin, hurried after them as they all approached the shop. Unlocking the door, I ushered everyone inside then closed up again.

"Hey everyone. Take a seat wherever you like. Who wants coffee and who prefers tea? As it happens, we have both on hand," I joked.

"Tea for me," Colleen and Barb both ordered.

"I need a strong cup of coffee," remarked Aunt Fran.

"Me too," said Carol.

"Okay, coming right up," I said as I dashed to the kitchen.

Anna and I carried the tray of drinks and pastries from the kitchen. After serving everyone, we joined them for a well-deserved break before starting the meeting.

"Who's watching the store?" I asked my Aunt Fran as I munched on a cherry Danish then sipped my tea. "Ah, that's so good."

"Mmm, Betty as usual. I'm so lucky to have her; she practically runs the place some days. Especially now with the campaign keeping me so busy." Fran took a swallow of the hot coffee.

"Okay. Shall we get down to it?" Colleen asked as she pulled a notebook and pen from her purse.

Colleen Callahan Wythe flicked her shoulder-length auburn hair behind her ears and looked expectantly at us. Colleen, with her Irish emerald-green eyes and sprinkle of freckles across her nose, looked so pretty and fragile that most people made the mistake of not taking her seriously. Being friends since children and throughout our college years, I knew better to never underestimate my friend. I'm sure the teachers and students at the Meadowood Elementary School, where Colleen presided as principal, also knew her soft-spoken commands were meant to be followed. Now she took control of my aunt's mayoral campaign in her organized and methodical manner.

"Tonight's debate will be critical. Fran must explain her vision for the town and provide a sharp contrast to Donald Dickson's past record and her future plans for Meadowood. You're both small business owners ... you with the dress shop and Dickson runs the pharmacy. You're both members of the Chamber of Commerce but that's as far as the similarities go. We need to show voters the important differences that are key to our town's future."

I clapped my hands and grinned at my friend. "Maybe you should make the campaign speeches!"

"She's right. People need to learn the difference between Fran and Dickson. The man is up to something. I have it on good authority that scalawag's scheming to bring in some mining company to our region. That worries me," said Anna in her western twang as she sat back in her chair and crossed her arms. At times like this, when riled up, Anna's Texan roots and western drawl became more obvious.

"What good authority? I've heard rumors too but haven't been able to confirm the facts," Fran said.

"Teresa Maxwell at Cut and Curl told me she heard about Dickson's idea to allow fracking outside of town from Polly Ames. Polly works as a part-time housekeeper for Adele Dickson. Polly over heard it first hand when she was dusting in the parlor and the mayor was talking on the phone. Naturally she told Teresa." Anna nodded her head as if that proved the information was legitimate. After all, everyone knew that the hairdresser held the rank of biggest gossip in town. If you wanted to know the latest news, you asked Teresa.

Barb and Carol both laughed at Anna describing the circuitous route of gossip but agreed it was likely gospel.

"If Polly heard Dickson talk about fracking on the phone, he must be confident that he's got the deal in the bag. What does he have to gain by a mining company drilling for coal or gas? Sounds like a potential payoff or cut of the profits. I'll try to learn more," I said as we all nodded in agreement about Dickson's shady plan.

"What do you need us to do, Colleen? Carol and I can put up posters or make phone calls. Just say the word," Barb offered.

"I need you gals to plaster the town in posters. Let's see Andrews for Mayor announcements right next to the bicentennial banners on every store front. On parade day, hand out campaign buttons to every spectator. When it gets closer to election day, we'll all make phone calls to remind people to get out and vote for Fran Andrews," Colleen said.

Finishing my cup of tea, I glanced at my aunt. She'd make a great mayor. I felt so proud of her.

Frances Andrews, my mother's sister, was an attractive widow who owned and operated the best dress shop in Meadowood called Frannie's Frocks. Fran had left her California home and returned to Meadowood following her husband's death, some thirty years ago. She worked on annual food drives and whatever committees in town needed her energy. Plus, she generously invested in the A&M Tea Shop to help her favorite niece. I loved my aunt dearly; at times, I felt closer to her than my mother and not just because we favored each other with our dark blonde hair and blue eyes. The only difference in our appearance was the handful of gray strands in her hair and the extra pounds curving my hips and thighs. My aunt was almost twenty years my senior, but slimmer and more physically active than me. She was a force to be reckoned with and hard to match.

I rose to carry my tea cup into the kitchen. Eyeing my circle of friends, I asked, "Anyone want a refill?"

Judging by the shake of heads, I gathered up the other empty cups and headed for the kitchen. Fran followed me.

"Hey, I just wanted to ask you ... you're okay with me using Colleen as my campaign manager, right? You know I love you dearly and think you'd do a great job, but honestly you've got so much on your plate now, I didn't want to burden you. I know you've been helping on the parade preparations and the bicentennial committee plus busy with your cub scout den. What with splitting your time between the tea shop, scouts, committees, and a full home life with two young boys and husband—well, I don't know how you manage as it is." Fran laid a hand on my arm and searched my eyes for understanding.

"Don't worry. Colleen is ideal as your manager; she's got the summer off from school and there's no one more organized and dedicated. You made the right choice. I'll do everything that I can to assist her. I don't feel slighted in the least."

"Thank you, Merry. I was concerned you might think I didn't consider you capable, far from it. If anyone in Meadowood knows how to get things done, it's you; well maybe right behind me, of course! Must be a family trait," laughed Aunt Fran.

We hugged each other, then returned to the tea room to hear Colleen repeat the debate starting time.

"We should be at the Oak Meadow Inn before seven o'clock."

"Sounds like a plan. See you all there," said Fran.

www.ingramcontent.com/pod-product-compliance
Lightning Source LLC
Chambersburg PA
CBHW071529100726
47908CB00004B/1342